The
Mysterious
Passover Visitors

The Mysterious Passover Visitors

ANN BIXBY HEROLD

Illustrated by
Mary Chambers

HERALD PRESS
Scottdale, Pennsylvania
Kitchener, Ontario

Library of Congress Cataloging-in-Publication Data

Herold, Ann Bixby.
    The mysterious Passover visitors / Ann Bixby Herold ; illustrated
by Mary Chambers.
        p.   cm.
    Summary: A young boy, living in Roman-occupied Jerusalem, is
determined to stay up and see the mysterious visitors who have
arranged to celebrate Passover in his mother's house.
    ISBN 0-8361-3494-X (alk. paper) :
    [1. Jesus Christ—Fiction.   2. Jerusalem—Fiction.   3. Passover-
-Fiction.]   I. Chambers, Mary, ill.   II. Title.
PZ7.H4319My   1989
[Fic]—dc19   89-1946
                                                                          CIP
                                                                          AC

The paper used in this publication meets the minimum requirements
of American National Standard for Information Sciences—Per-
manence of Paper for Printed Library Materials, ANSI Z39.48-1984.

Scripture is quoted or adapted from the *Holy Bible: New International Version.* Copyright © 1973, 1978, 1984 by the International
Bible Society. Used by Permission of Zondervan Bible Publishers.

THE MYSTERIOUS PASSOVER VISITORS
Copyright © 1989 by Herald Press, Scottdale, Pa. 15683
    Published simultaneously in Canada by Herald Press,
    Kitchener, Ont. N2G 4M5. All rights reserved.
Library of Congress Catalog Card Number: 89-1946
International Standard Book Number: 0-8361-3494-X
Printed in the United States of America
Design by Paula M. Johnson

95 94 93 92 91 90 89 10 9 8 7 6 5 4 3 2 1

To Ray Hall,
who gave me the idea,
and to Marlene

Contents

1
Sign of the Water Jar

IT WAS A MYSTERY from the very beginning, and John Mark loved mysteries.

"I want you to stay in the courtyard this morning," his mother told him. "Someone is coming to see me. When you hear a knock at the gate, you are to let the man in and bring him to me."

"What man?"

"I don't know his name."

"A stranger? Why is he coming here? What does he want?" The questions tumbled out. John Mark's mother raised her eyes to heaven.

"Not another day of endless questions," she sighed.

John Mark slipped his arm around her waist.

"I only want to know what is going on," he said with a hopeful grin.

She shook her head and laughed.

"Cleaning," she said. "Housecleaning is what is going on. Outside with you, John Mark, and do as I ask."

John Mark whiled away the time sitting in a patch of sun next to his mother's sweet-smelling jasmine bush. It was quiet and peaceful in the courtyard with the gate to the street closed. Too peaceful. After the first eager moments of waiting, John Mark grew bored. He watched the honeybees buzzing around the jasmine flowers. He mended the leather strap of one of his sandals. He drew pictures with his finger in the sandy dirt. He closed his eyes and daydreamed.

The hours passed. The shadows on the far side of the courtyard grew shorter, but still there was no knock at the gate.

I wish he would hurry, John Mark thought as he picked at a scab on his knee.

Beyond the thick, mud wall he could hear the people of Jerusalem going about their business. Normally, on a holiday like this, when there was no school, John Mark would have been out in the narrow streets. Jerusalem was exciting at Passover.

The sun was hot. It was making him feel drowsy. He got to his feet and stretched.

There is no reason I can't wait outside the gate, he decided. He wondered why he hadn't thought of it earlier. The time would pass much more quickly watching the crowds go by.

The knock came as he was crossing the courtyard. It sounded urgent. John Mark ran over to the door in the gateway and threw it open.

The man standing there was out of breath.

"Come in," John Mark said eagerly.

With a quick glance over his shoulder, the stranger stepped inside.

"Close the door," he ordered. "And take me to the owner of this house."

10

"Follow me," John Mark said. "I'll call my mother."

Every nerve in John Mark's body was tingling. What could the stranger want with them? He was determined to find out.

When his mother came out of the house, John Mark moved behind her, hoping she would forget he was there. She turned and looked at him.

"Go up to the roof, John Mark. Bring down the sheets Rhoda put out to air."

That was strange, for she hardly ever asked him to fetch the sheets.

She wants me out of the way, he thought as he bounded up the outside staircase. He scooped up the sheets, warm from the sun. He almost tripped over them in his hurry to get back downstairs.

He heard his mother say, "You will find some empty water jars in the storeroom under the stairs."

"I only need one," the man said.

John Mark ran indoors and dropped the sheets on the sleeping platform. When he came out, the man was heading for the gate with an empty water jar under his arm. John Mark watched, openmouthed, as his mother let the man out. A man going for water? Didn't he care what people would think of him? How foolish he would look when he joined the women at the well!

"Why didn't you send Rhoda for water?" he asked as the man disappeared into the crowded street. "It is women's work and Rhoda is our maidservant."

To his surprise, a look of fear crossed his mother's face. She closed the door and leaned against it.

"Hush!" she whispered. "Don't speak so loudly. Someone might hear you." She caught hold of his arm and pulled him toward the house. "You must stop asking me about that man, John Mark. It is not of my doing. I was told to send him."

"Told to send him?" his whisper echoed hers. "Somebody told you to send a man to the well?" It didn't make sense.

"He hasn't gone for water."

"Then why did he take a water jar?"

"It is a sign."

"The jar? What kind of a sign?" they had reached the house door. John Mark shook himself free and ran his fingers through his dark curly hair. Why was she talking in riddles? What was going on?

"A sign that they are to follow him. They are to look for a man carrying a water jar. He will lead them here."

"Lead *who* here? Who are *they*? Why won't you tell me?" John Mark thumped the wall with his fist and flakes of dried mud fell to the step.

"Stop that!" His mother's dark eyes flashed a warning.

"I'm sorry. *Please* tell me," he pleaded.

Pleading didn't work either. All she said was, "I am too busy to answer your questions. Find Rhoda for me. Tell her I need her help in the guest room upstairs. There is a lot of work to be done, so hurry."

John Mark found Rhoda gossiping under a neighbor's grapevine. He gave her the message and they walked home together. His mother was already in the upper room. He followed Rhoda up the staircase.

"Are you cleaning the room for a meeting?" he asked from the doorway. His mother sometimes rented out the upstairs room. She shook her head.

"What for, then?" He stepped onto the end of a mat,

Rhoda swatted him with her broom.

just as she bent to pick it up.

"Move," she ordered.

Rhoda swatted him with her broom. He backed away and asked again, "What for?"

"For a Passover feast," his mother said.

"Ours?" he asked, puzzled. Their Passover meal was usually served in the family quarters downstairs. Besides, this year their celebration was going to be different. Because none of their family could come to Jerusalem, they had been invited to a friend's house.

"You said we were going to eat with Benjamin and Ruth," he reminded his mother. "Are they coming here instead?"

"No."

"Then whose feast is it?"

She carried the mat out onto the flat roof and shook it. On her way back in, she said, "What did I say about asking questions, John Mark? Have you nothing to do? Either help us move these cushions, or go away."

The Passover feast must have something to do with the mysterious people who are willing to follow a man with a water jug, he thought as he picked up a cushion. But why couldn't they arrive like normal guests? All they had to do was find the right street and ask which house belongs to Mary. Who *were* they?

John Mark couldn't bear the agony of not knowing. He put the cushion down and said, "The feast is for the people that stranger is bringing here."

It was a statement, not a question. When his mother flashed a warning glance at Rhoda, he knew he was right.

The surge of triumph was overwhelmed by an even

bigger surge of anger. Rhoda knew!

Why would she tell Rhoda, and not me? he thought.

"If Father were alive he would tell me," he blurted out. "Father trusted me, even if you don't."

He saw the look of distress in his mother's eyes, but he was too angry to be sorry. When she came over and put her hands on his shoulders, he pulled away.

"It was nothing to do with trusting you, John Mark," she said quietly. "I wanted to protect you. It is because I love you . . . ." Her voice trailed away and she sighed. "In these dangerous times, the less you know about such things, the better."

"What *things?*" Even the smallest child knew the times were dangerous. A boy on the edge of manhood knew it best of all. "Why won't you tell me? Father would expect me to help you, but how can I, when you won't tell me anything? Why do you always treat me like a child?"

"I don't know," she admitted. "Each time I put my hands on your shoulders, I must reach higher. It is foolish of me not to realize you will soon be grown up. If I tell you who is coming here, will you promise to tell no one, not even Samuel?"

Samuel was John Mark's closest friend. He was the only one John Mark would want to tell, but he was away. He had gone to spend the Passover holiday at his grandparent's house on the other side of the city, so the promise would be easy to keep.

"Samuel is away," he told her. "He won't be home for three days."

"I want your word that you won't tell anybody else."

"I promise."

"Come closer. We mustn't speak above a whisper," she said, even though it was impossible for anyone to overhear them. "The men who are coming here are followers of Jesus of Nazareth."

"The Rabbi Jesus? The one who wrecked the temple courtyard? The Teacher who chased the moneylenders away?" John Mark gasped.

She nodded. "That is why we are keeping it a secret. He is coming here too, but not until later. He and his friends are going to eat their Passover meal in our guest room."

"Why here?"

"Because they asked me. Because I am sympathetic to the danger the Rabbi is in. I have seen him heal sick people, John Mark."

"I didn't know that," he said with surprise. "You never told me."

She smiled and shook her head. "How many boys listen to their mother's talk?" she teased. Her smile vanished, and she looked worried. "Everyone in Jerusalem knows the chief priests want to arrest him. They haven't managed it so far, but his followers are on their guard. The fewer people who know he is coming here tonight, the better for him. And for us."

Now I understand! John Mark thought with a shiver of excitement. It was true. Everyone in the city knew that Caiaphas, the high priest, and the priests and elders of the Temple wanted to get rid of Jesus of Nazareth. Ever since he had ridden into Jerusalem in triumph they had hated him. People had thrown down their cloaks for the Rabbi. They had waved palm branches and leaves. Some had even cried, "Hosanna to the Son of David!

Blessed is he who comes in the name of the Lord! Hosanna in the highest!" as if he were a king, instead of the son of a carpenter from Nazareth.

To the temple authorities, such a man meant trouble with Rome. Rome ruled Israel. Under the Romans the priests had kept their power because they had promised to control the people. If the Nazarene, or anybody else, led a revolt against the Roman army of occupation, they would be blamed. And so, as Jesus of Nazareth became more and more popular, they plotted against him.

Everyone knew why Caiaphas hadn't arrested him. He was so popular, his arrest would cause a riot.

The chief priests were getting desperate. When Jesus preached in the temple courtyards, they tried to trick him into saying something against the Jewish laws. He always outwitted them. It made them hate him more than ever.

They could do nothing but watch and wait. Even after he overturned the moneylender's tables, they were afraid to arrest him.

As John Mark watched his mother and Rhoda clean the upper room, he wished he had paid more attention to Jesus of Nazareth.

I thought he was just another man claiming to be a prophet, but he must be different, he thought. He is afraid of no one. Not Caiaphas. Not the Romans. Maybe he *is* the leader Israel has been waiting for. The man sent by God to free us from the Romans, be our king, and lead us to glory!

Another shiver of excitement shot down John Mark's spine. To think that tonight he will be eating supper at our house!

2
Zeal of the Rabbi

IS THE RABBI JESUS going to stay overnight?" John Mark asked his mother.

"I don't think so," she replied. "The message said he wanted a room where he and his friends could share the Passover feast. It didn't say anything about staying the night. I will know more when his followers get here."

"How many are coming?"

"I don't know that either."

"If they want to sleep here I'll keep watch," he offered eagerly. "If I put my sleeping mat across the stairs . . . ."

"No, John Mark."

"At least let me ask them."

"The answer is *no*," she said firmly. "They have asked to be left alone and we will respect their wishes. Now please go away so we can finish our cleaning."

"Just one more question and I will leave you in peace." John Mark clung stubbornly to the doorpost.

She laughed and shook her head. "Peace? With you around? You are impossible, my son. Why must you pester everyone with your endless questions?"

"If I pester, it is only because no one will answer them."

"That's not true."

"Then why won't you answer this one?"

"What is it?" She sighed and brushed some dust from the skirt of her blue wool gown.

"When will the Nazarene be here? I don't want to miss him. I've only ever seen him at a distance before."

"Didn't you hear a word I said?" his mother cried. "He has asked to be left alone."

"I won't get in his way. I won't say a word to him. I only want to see what he looks like, that's all. I'll be so quiet nobody will notice me."

Rhoda let out a hoot of laughter. "There is small chance of that, John Mark. Can a body ignore a thorn in its side?"

"A thorn? Me?"

"You," she retorted. "Maybe you would prefer to be compared to a stone in a sandal, or an ache in a tooth."

"I don't know what you mean, Rhoda," he said.

"Oh yes, you do. You are like a honeybee. All that buzz, buzz, buzz for one tiny drop of honey. You may make our lives sweeter, but oh, the noise while you are doing it!"

His mother nodded, but she was smiling. John Mark smiled too, although he tried not to. Rhoda had been with his family longer than he could remember, and she loved to tease him. He crossed his eyes and bared his teeth at her.

"Bees sting," he said. "Watch out!"

"So do old hornets like me," was her quick reply. "Hornets are bigger than bees and their stings are sharper, so *you* watch out!"

She walked over and flapped her apron at him. The dust made him cough, but he refused to move.

"Mother still hasn't answered my question," he complained. "When will Jesus of Nazareth be here?"

His mother sank onto a couch and put her head in her hands.

"Will you never give up?" she cried. "What am I to do with you?"

"You could trade me for Jacob," he suggested cheerfully. "He hardly ever opens his mouth. Maybe you would prefer him and his gloomy silences."

"It would be a change," she sighed.

"That's for sure, mistress," Rhoda agreed. "Remember last week when you sent me to help Jacob's mother with her new baby? The boy didn't say a word the whole time I was there. I can't tell you what a relief it was not to be interrupted every few moments. What if he does look miserable. At least he is quiet, God be praised."

John Mark grinned. "That's strange, Rhoda. Yesterday I overheard you telling a neighbor you like me because I am so full of life. I didn't hear you say a word about wishing I was quiet."

Rhoda turned away to hide a smile. "You think I would complain about you when I work for your family? Besides, if I told people the truth about how many questions you ask, nobody would believe me."

"There is something to be said for peace and quiet, John Mark," Mother said. "*Please* go away."

"Tell me when the Rabbi is coming and I'll go."

"Will you promise not to bother him?"

"I won't say a word to him."

"Or his followers?"

"I will only speak to them if they speak to me first."

With a sigh, his mother gave in. "The messenger said the Rabbi will be here at sundown," she told him. "The men who are coming here now are going to get everything ready."

She stood up, picked up a broom, and prodded him with the handle.

"That is the very last thing I am going to tell you, John Mark. Now *go*."

He backed out onto the flat roof and stared down at the courtyard. An almond tree in full bloom dropped its pinkish-white petals on the sandy earth. There was a grape arbor too, and a thick trunked olive tree. Beyond the sunbaked mud wall, John Mark could see the crowded street. Passover visitors strolled by, followed by noisy street sellers vying for their attention. John Mark could hardly wait for sundown. At last he was going to see, up close, the most exciting Passover visitor of all. The man who had caused all the trouble in the temple courtyard.

How I wish I had been there! he thought.

Everyone in the city knew the moneylenders cheated people. The sellers of animals were no better. On his last visit to Jerusalem from Cana in Galilee, John Mark's uncle had been cheated by a lamb seller when he went to the temple to make a sacrifice. He knew he had been cheated, but he didn't dare say anything because the lambs belonged to the family of Annas, a former high priest.

Besides lambs, there were always pigeons and doves for sale, as well as kids and oxen. The birds and animals had to be perfect if they were to be used as sacrifices. The priest used that as an excuse to stop people from bringing their own from home or from buying them in the city. Of course there were plenty of perfect, unblemished animals for sale outside the temple, but the priests didn't make any money on those. That is why they banned them.

As John Mark stood on the roof and watched the people pass by, he remembered seeing a man try to take a dove into the temple. The guards at the gate had refused to let him in. They had told him to get rid of the dove and buy one inside. The man had told him the dove was perfect. He had asked them to examine it for blemishes, but they had refused. When he tried to argue with them, they had chased him away.

John Mark had missed the wrecking of the temple courtyard by only a few moments. He and Samuel were walking along a street below the temple when it happened. The first sign of anything unusual was a cloud of doves in the sky above the towering walls.

"I wonder where they came from?" said Samuel.

"Let's go and find out," suggested John Mark.

They started to run. As they came closer, they heard shouts. The boys headed for the nearest gate. They were almost there when a flood of lambs and goats came pouring out. Men were chasing them. As passersby stopped to watch, the men tried to round up the animals and shepherd them back inside. Overhead, the doves were still circling.

The shouting and the bleating and the baaing drew a crowd. The noise also drew the temple guards. When John Mark and Samuel had tried to go into the courtyard they were turned away.

It wasn't until later that they heard the whole story. Jerusalem was abuzz with tales of moneylenders crawling around in the dust looking for spilled coins. Of overturned tables and chairs. Of sellers chasing animals around the courtyard. Of Jesus of Nazareth crying, "It is written, 'My house will be called a house of prayer for all nations.' But you have made it a den of robbers!"

No one felt sorry for the moneylenders. All over the city people cheered. At the temple, Caiaphas and the chief priests were angrier than ever.

"The Nazarene has given them one more reason to hate him," the people of Jerusalem said among themselves. "He had better be careful."

If the people thought the Rabbi Jesus would stay away from the temple, they were mistaken. He was back in the courtyard the next day as if he had nothing in the world to be afraid of.

It was then that John Mark started to wonder if Jesus of Nazareth were a Zealot. The Zealots were bands of hot-tempered men who refused to pay taxes to the Romans. They claimed to be zealous for God and his rule. But they were always planning trouble and talking of war.

As John Mark waited on the roof, he thought about Zealots. If Jesus were one, his followers would be Zealots too. It wasn't like his mother to invite such men to her house. She didn't like Zealots at all. She thought they were troublemakers.

Maybe I had better warn her, he thought. She won't like it if they plan war on the Romans while they are here.

He was about to go and talk to her when Rhoda came out of the guest room. She gave him a look that said, "Stay away!" as she went down the stairs. He could hear his mother fussing over the seating arrangements.

23

I'll wait until I've seen the men before I say anything, he decided.

The midday sun was hot. Under his brown wool robe John Mark could feel a trickle of sweat between his shoulder blades. He moved to a patch of shade cast by a neighbor's house higher up the hill.

I wish Samuel hadn't gone away, he thought. He'll never believe me when he hears who came to our house today! I wish he would come home early so I could tell. . . . With a twinge of guilt, he remembered his mother's words.

"Tell no one, not even Samuel," she had said, and he had promised.

3
At the Market

WHEN THE MAN with the water jar came back there were two strangers following him. The man opened the door in the gateway without stopping to knock and slipped into the courtyard. John Mark saw him put down the jar and beckon to the two men. As soon as they were safely inside he left, closing the door behind him.

From the roof, John Mark watched the two men approach the downstairs door. Up close they didn't look at all dangerous or wild. He was disappointed.

As he stared down at the visitors, his mother came out of the house. They greeted her and he heard one of them say, "Our Master says, 'Where is the room where I may eat the Passover with my disciples?'"

"Follow me," she said.

Halfway up the staircase the man said, "I am Peter, and this is John. We are fishermen from the Sea of Galilee."

John Mark wasn't surprised to hear they were fishermen. Both of them had the bright eyes and sunburned faces of men who work outdoors. With their powerful, broad shoulders, they looked nothing like most of the men he knew, pale-faced city men who spent their lives bent over work-benches in the open-fronted shops that lined the streets.

"This is my son, John Mark," Mother said when they reached the roof. "Here is our guest room. Will it be big enough?"

The men nodded to John Mark and followed her inside. They left the door ajar, and he went closer to listen.

"How many will you be?" he heard his mother ask.

"Twelve plus our Master," said the man called John. "I'm sure there will be room enough for us to eat in comfort."

"What about the meal?" Mother asked. "What do you need?"

"Everything," said the man called Peter. "We have nothing with us. We will need bitter herbs, salt, vegetables, wine, unleavened bread."

"If you will help me rid the house of leaven, I will bake the unleavened bread." Mother offered. "Do you want me to roast the lamb too?"

Peter nodded. "How much time will you need to cook it?"

"If you want to eat soon after sundown, we shouldn't waste time. Who will go to the temple and make the sacrifice?"

"We will. We are to meet somebody there. Now that we know how to find your house, we will leave straightaway."

"Is it safe for you to enter the temple?" Mother asked. "What if the priests recognize you as followers of Jesus of Nazareth?"

"Don't worry yourself," said John. "It has all been arranged."

"But. . . ."

"The courtyards will be overflowing with pilgrims," said Peter. "Do we look different from other men?"

"No. But your Galilean accents might give you away."

"We'll keep quiet," John promised.

To John Mark's surprise, the other man chuckled, "I can only promise to try," he said. "I'm not known for my silence."

John Mark, peering around the door, saw John smile and nod.

"We will be back as soon as we have sacrificed a lamb," he said.

"All will be ready," Mother promised. "Are you sure you will be able to find your way back here?"

Before the men could answer, John Mark pushed open the door. "Would you like me to go with you?" he offered eagerly.

Too late he remembered the promise he had made to his mother. He blushed guiltily as he avoided her eyes.

The men were staring at him.

"If you want something to do, John Mark, you can go to market with Rhoda." His mother's voice was quiet, but there was no mistaking the look on her face. Or the angry way she pushed back a stray lock of dark hair. "If she is to buy enough food and wine for thirteen hungry men, she will need help to carry it home."

Shopping with Rhoda! John Mark swallowed his disappointment. If he showed he was willing, maybe they would let him help serve the meal later. It would be a good way to get a close look at the man from Nazareth.

He stayed up on the roof while his mother and the visitors made the ceremonial search for leaven. They had to gather up all the everyday bread they could find.

Even leftover crusts must be removed from the house. No such bread could be kept or eaten over the Passover holiday. Flat unleavened bread would be eaten instead. Unleavened bread was made especially for the feast. It was baked to remind the Jews of their ancestors and their escape from Egypt, when there had been no time to cook meals or bake the usual kind of bread.

As soon as the search was over, Peter and John set out for the temple. From the roof, John Mark watched them go. His eyes scanned the street beyond the courtyard wall. Was anyone waiting to follow them? It didn't look like it, but with the street so crowded, it was hard to tell.

"John Mark?" His mother was calling to him from the downstairs doorway.

"Find Rhoda," she told him. "Ask her to go to the storeroom and bring out bowls and cups for thirteen people. If there aren't enough, we will have to borrow some. Tell her they must all be washed and taken upstairs. When that is done, the two of you can go to market. Tell her there isn't much time. Our visitors want to eat as soon as the sun goes down."

The market had been open since dawn. By the time Rhoda and John Mark got there, it was afternoon. In the section where the food was sold, the stalls were half empty.

"These people are like a cloud of locusts who gobble up everything in sight," Rhoda grumbled.

She elbowed her way over to a stall that still had some vegetables for sale. John Mark struggled along behind her, pushed this way and that by the good-natured holiday crowd. When he caught up, she was picking over a pile of wilted lettuce and chicory.

"Look at this," she complained. "Early morning is the time for marketing. Only fools pay money for food spoiled by the midday sun."

At a stall shaded by a striped awning she picked out some parsley and got into an argument over the price. John Mark groaned. Was there anything more boring than shopping for food?

"Buy something and let's go home," he muttered in her ear.

She frowned. "You can't hurry the buying of food, John Mark. Not when it is for guests. You will have to be patient."

"I'll wait for you over by the perfume stalls," he said. "The crowd is thinner there."

She nodded. "Stay there. I'll come for you when my basket is full."

There were hardly any people around the perfume stalls. John Mark relaxed. The mingled scents of the perfumes was a lot more pleasant than the sour smell of closely packed bodies. From where he stood he could see Rhoda's basket. It was balanced on her head. As he stared at it, a hand appeared. The hand was holding a lettuce. Rhoda was waving the lettuce around in the air, pretending she was going to toss it into her basket, then changing her mind. John Mark grinned. He knew she must be giving the stall holder a fierce argument about the price. His mother always said Rhoda was the best bargain hunter in the whole of Jerusalem.

The lettuce was tossed into the basket and Rhoda moved on. Soon John Mark couldn't see any sign of her. He waited and waited, and still she didn't come. He was about to go and look for her when he heard a voice say, "This perfume is imported from Egypt."

The seller at the nearest stall was showing a tiny alabaster flask to two Roman officers. Their crested helmets brushed the awning and made the men look like giants.

"Buy some perfume for your wives, for your sweethearts," the seller implored them.

The officers ignored him. The tallest one whispered something in his friend's ear. They both burst out laughing and turned away, their red capes swinging.

As John Mark watched them, he was filled with a mixture of admiration and hatred. He admired the proud way they wore their uniforms, but he hated what those uniforms stood for. His father had told him that every Roman soldier on the streets of Jerusalem was a reminder that Israel was a conquered nation.

He remembered the conversation they had had just before his father fell ill and died. Father had said that if the Jews would stop quarreling among themselves and stand together, they would be able to stand up to the Romans and force them to leave Israel.

"We need to support each other, not argue over unimportant things," he told John Mark. "A strong leader would unite us. Look at the Romans. They are united under their Caesar. That is why they have conquered the world. They are proud of what they stand for. Well, we Jews are proud too. We are God's chosen people, but sometimes you would never know it."

It was true what his father said about the Romans, John Mark thought as he watched the officers walk away. The market was packed with people, yet no one stood in their way. Nobody elbowed them or pushed them around. As if commanded by some unseen hand, a path opened to let them through the crowd.

If I were wearing a Roman officer's uniform, Rhoda's basket would be full by now, he thought. No one would dare overcharge her. I would put my hand on my sword, and that would be that.

He straightened his back as he imagined himself dressed in full armor, a helmet with a plume, and a bright red cloak. It certainly would be a change from the short, brown robe he was wearing. His fingers touched the worn leather belt around his waist. The belt was much too big, but he wouldn't exchange it for King Herod's robes. It had belonged to his father and he wore it every day.

A uniform would make me look older, he said to himself.

Flies were buzzing around his head. He swatted at them with his hand and turned to look at the perfume stalls. A pretty girl in a sky-blue robe was buying some perfume.

"Why don't *you* buy some too?" a familiar voice whispered in John Mark's ear. "It will make you smell better. A boy who smells like a goat is an offense to everyone he meets."

Samuel was standing behind him, flashing his familiar broken-toothed grin. John Mark had been with him when he broke his teeth falling off a wall.

"Samuel! What happened? Why aren't you at your grandparent's house?"

"My mother sent me home for her cooking pots," Samuel explained. "More visitors arrived than they expected." He made a face. "It is terrible there, John Mark.

The house is full of crying babies. I must have the biggest family in Israel. You don't know how lucky you are to be able to sleep alone at night. Last night I didn't close my eyes once with all the coughing and the scratching. When one person turned over, we all had to turn over. It's not funny," he said when John Mark laughed. "There are more people packed into that house than olives in an olive jar."

"If you were sent home for your mother's pots, what are you doing here?" John Mark asked.

"Wasting time so I won't have to go back. Why are *you* here?"

"Mother made me come. There will be too much for Rhoda to carry with the wine and everything," John Mark said without thinking.

Samuel looked puzzled. "You said your Passover was going to be quiet this year. Why do you need so much food and wine?"

"It's not for us."

"Who, then?"

John Mark hesitated. He knew he could trust his friend to keep the secret. But if he told Samuel who the food was for, he would want to see Jesus of Nazareth too.

I know Samuel, John Mark thought. He won't be able to stay away. Mother knows he is supposed to be at his grandparent's house, so she'll know I broke my promise.

"Are you having visitors after all?" Samuel asked curiously.

John Mark took a deep breath. It was such a hard secret to keep!

"I . . . my. . . ."

"John Mark!" One hand raised to stop the basket from slipping from her head, a breathless Rhoda planted herself between the two boys. She turned her back on Samuel and stared hard at John Mark. "We must hurry," she said. Her voice was heavy with meaning. "We have a lot of work to do."

John Mark's legs went weak with relief. Rhoda had saved him. Telling Samuel would only have led to trouble.

"I'll see you after the holiday, Samuel," he said. A fly had settled on his arm and he slapped at it. When it flew away he pretended he was trying to catch it. He didn't dare look at Samuel.

"Come, John Mark," said Rhoda.

As he followed her into the crowd, he glanced over his shoulder. Samuel was staring after them. From the look on his face, John Mark knew exactly what he was thinking: What was it Rhoda stopped you from telling me, John Mark?

4

Are They Zealots?

JOHN MARK AND RHODA were welcomed home by the delicious smell of roasting meat. The lamb was on a spit over an open fire. Drops of fat fell spluttering and hissing into the flames below. John Mark's mother, her arms dusty with flour, was making the unleavened bread. On a flat-topped rock were two freshly baked round, flat loaves.

Rhoda emptied the basket and John Mark carried a jar of wine and a jar of water up the staircase. There was a pleasant breeze up on the roof. The sun was working its way down the afternoon sky and soon it would be cooler.

The two men were sitting in the upper room, talking in low voices. The one called Peter was shaking his head and frowning. When he saw John Mark in the doorway, he put his hand on his friend's arm.

John Mark could tell by their faces that they were annoyed at being interrupted. In the uneasy silence that followed, he said, "I've brought a jar of water. And the wine."

"Good," said the man called John. "I'm thirsty."

The jars were getting heavier and heavier. John Mark hesitated, not sure if he should go in.

Peter's frown deepened.

"Come in. Come in." His voice was quick with impatience. "Must we beg you for a cool drink of water?" He picked up two cups and held them out.

His frown lasted until John Mark had put down the jars and filled the cups with water. Then, so quickly it was startling, it was replaced by a warm smile.

"That was good," he said when he had drained his cup.

As John Mark refilled it, he noticed Peter's hands for the first time. They were covered with scars. Peter saw him staring. He held out a hand, palm up.

"They are rope burns," he explained. "The brand of a fisherman. A life of battling storms of the Sea of Galilee has left its mark on me. On John too. We don't tend nets anymore, but we will never lose the marks of our profession."

"Do you miss your fishing boats?" John Mark asked curiously. Growing up in a crowded city, he had often dreamed of sailing over sparkling water, a cool fresh breeze at his back.

The men exchanged glances and shook their heads.

"Our Master says we are to be fishers of men from now on," John told him.

"Fishers of men? What does that mean?" John Mark asked.

"We are to cast our nets for men instead of fish," said John.

When John Mark looked puzzled. Peter said, "We are to battle storms of another kind. Much more powerful storms."

"Are you Zealots?" The question was out before he could stop it. "Are you going to raise an army and fight the Romans and throw them out of our country?"

Peter looked startled. "You think I am a Zealot?" he cried. "Do I look like a Zealot? Act like one?"

"No, but I thought...." John Mark's face was burning.

"One of our number, Simon, *was* a Zealot," John said. "Not any longer. Our Master does not agree with the Zealots. His message is one of love and forgiveness."

That wasn't the message of the Zealots, John Mark knew. They wanted war, not love. But what about the business with the moneylenders?

"Didn't Jesus of Nazareth overturn the tables in the temple courtyard?" he asked.

Peter stared at him through narrowed eyes.

"With reason! Aren't the moneylenders known to be robbers?" he demanded. "Don't the sellers of animals cheat people?"

"Yes," said John Mark. "Everybody knows that."

"You were at market today," John said to him. "Tell me, is there any difference between the marketplace and the temple courtyard? Aren't there stalls in both places selling overpriced goods?"

"Yes."

"That's the shame of it!" growled Peter. "At least the sellers in the market are there to earn money to live, not line the pockets of temple officials. To think they make money from poor people in our holiest place! They squat in the only temple area where other nations may come and pray—if they aren't crowded out! No wonder our Master was angry."

He looked so fierce John Mark took a step back.

"Peter hates injustice, as we all do," John said when

**He noticed Peter's hands for the first time.
They were covered with scars.**

Peter lapsed into a glowering silence. "Have you heard our Master preach, John Mark?"

"No, I haven't."

John Mark didn't tell him there were more interesting things for a boy to do in a busy city like Jerusalem. That until recently he had ignored the talk about the man from Nazareth because he thought he was just another long-winded teacher claiming to be a prophet and a healer. Why is your master different from all the rest? he thought, and wondered if he dared ask the question out loud.

Peter stood up and paced around the room. He stopped in front of John Mark and fixed his bright eyes upon him.

"What do you think should happen to those robbers in priest's robes? Perhaps you think they should be left alone. Perhaps you think our Master was wrong to turn them out. Would you want him to act like everybody else? All those downtrodden fools who let the priests steal money from them each time they go to the temple?"

He is talking to me as if I were a man, not a boy, John Mark thought. He was so surprised he forgot to be afraid of the big, rough fisherman.

John had noticed it too.

"You are talking to a boy, Peter," he said.

"So? Today's boy is tomorrow's man." Peter tugged at his beard and shrugged. "In a year he may be looking down at me instead of the other way around."

"But what can a boy know about such things?"

"He has eyes to see and ears to hear, hasn't he?" Peter roared. "Let him speak for himself."

John Mark's back had stiffened at John's words.

"I'm not stupid," he protested. "I like to learn. If I don't know something I always ask. I don't see why my. . . ." He caught himself just in time. The men were his mother's guests, and here he was arguing with them. It went against everything he had been taught about hospitality. His mother would be furious if she found out. "My mother says I ask too many questions," he added sheepishly.

Peter refilled his cup with water. When he looked up, the dark cloud had gone from his face.

"My mother said the same thing about me." He tugged at his beard and chuckled. "You thought we were Zealots?" His deep, rumbling laugh filled the room.

"Like me you are hot-tempered enough to be a Zealot," his friend said.

"That's true," Peter admitted. "We fishermen can be fiery, and I am one of the hottest. But my anger doesn't stay with me long. The Zealots live with their hatred night and day until it destroys them."

"Peter's anger is like a storm on the Sea of Galilee," John said. "Here one moment, so you fear for your life, and then it is gone. The sky is clear again, the water is calm, and you wonder if it was a bad dream."

Peter grinned and shrugged his broad shoulders. It was more like the grin of a guilty boy than a grown man.

"If only I could learn to think before I act," he sighed. "It would save me a lot of trouble."

John Mark's heart warmed toward him. Many times I've done something without stopping to think, he mused. How sorry I've been afterward. I know exactly how he feels. I like him. I like them both. I wish I knew more about them. What did John mean when he said they were to cast their nets for men, not fish? He was about to ask, when he heard his mother calling him.

As John Mark ran down the staircase he thought about the man the fishermen called Master. A man who fought against injustice and talked about love.

The mystery surrounding his mother's Passover visitors was growing all the time.

5

Look of a Prophet

BY SUNDOWN THE LAMB was cooked and ready to be eaten. Upstairs a lamp glowed in the dusk. Straw mats had been placed around the low table, but there weren't enough places for thirteen to recline at the meal. John Mark was told to go and borrow the rest from a neighbor.

"What shall I tell Sarah if she asks why we need them?" he worried.

"Just say they are for Passover," his mother told him. "It's better if she doesn't know who the meal is for, but if she finds out, the secret will be safe with her. Remember last year when her daughter Abigail suffered from that strange sleeping sickness? It was Jesus of Nazareth who cured her."

Of course! John Mark had forgotten about Abigail. The sleeping sickness had started when the little girl fell and hit her head while playing in the street. None of the physicians who examined her could waken her. When Sarah and her husband, Reuben had heard that the Nazarene was in Bethany healing people, they carried her there. When they brought her home, it was as if she had never been ill.

John Mark remembered that he and Samuel had not been impressed with the "miracle."

"Maybe she woke up by herself," Samuel had said, and John Mark agreed with him. The healing wasn't nearly as exciting as if Abigail had been cured of a withered leg, or demons.

Her family had sung the Rabbi's praises. Even now, a year later, they always went to hear him when he came to the city to preach.

"If you have to tell them, ask them to keep it a secret," Mother said to John Mark. "They will understand."

He needn't have worried. When he knocked at Sarah's door and asked to borrow the mats, all she said was "I suppose you'll be needing them for Passover."

"Yes," he replied. It was as easy as that.

John Mark was on his way home with an armful of mats when the Passover visitors arrived. The street was deserted. From behind closed doors came the familiar sounds of families settling down to eat.

Moving swiftly, their sandaled feet making no sound in the dust, the men loomed up out of the gathering darkness. John Mark watched them approach the house, and his heart beat faster.

Which one was Jesus of Nazareth? Was it the man in front, flanked by Peter and John?

John Mark reached the door in the gate first. He left it open and hurried across the courtyard and up the stairs. Panting, he burst into the upper room and put down the mats.

Outside, there were footsteps on the stairs.

"Welcome to our guest room," he heard his mother say. "Go in and make yourselves comfortable. I will send my maidservant to you with a bowl and towels for your handwashing. Tell her when you're ready to eat."

John Mark backed into the darkest corner.

Maybe Rhoda won't notice me, he thought. If she does I will offer to stay and help serve the meal.

When all thirteen men were inside the room, it was crowded. No one seemed to notice John Mark. He watched Peter and John welcome each man with a bearlike hug and a kiss.

They are like brothers, he thought.

He hid behind Peter's broad back when Rhoda came into the room. When Peter sat down, he hid behind another man. The men were taking their seats, one by one. To make matters worse, Rhoda lit two lamps and the darkness melted away.

When Rhoda bent to fill her bowl with water, John Mark ducked behind the cloaks that had been tossed into a pile. He waited a moment before lifting his head. Rhoda was offering the bowl to the man reclining in the place of honor.

That must be him! John Mark thought, hardly daring to breathe for fear someone would hear him.

The look of the man only added to the mystery. Growing up in Jerusalem, John Mark had heard and seen many so-called prophets. New ones were always appearing, claiming to have the answer to Israel's problems. The ones who preached the overthrow of Rome disappeared the quickest. The Roman governor saw to that. They were hauled away by his soldiers and flung into prison, never to be seen again. Others came, preached for a while, and moved on. When John Mark and his friends had nothing better to do, they would go and listen to the ramblings of the latest prophet. If there were hecklers in the crowd, it could even be fun.

43

Every prophet John Mark had ever seen had the same look in his eye. A strange, wild look.

"Why do they look like that?" he had once asked his father.

"It is the look of somebody who is hungry for power, my son," his father had told him. "Such men are all the same. They talk of restoring Israel to its former glory, but what they want is glory for themselves. Beware false prophets, John Mark."

"How can you tell a false prophet from a real one?" John Mark had wanted to know.

His father had frowned thoughtfully and run his fingers through his beard. "There is no easy answer to that question. All I can say is—beware! It is easy to tell lies. Easier, sometimes, than telling the truth."

"Isn't there a way to tell if a man is lying?"

"Not really."

"But if he leads a good life . . . .?"

"Alas, leading a good outward life is not always a sign of a good heart," Father sighed. "Look at some of our religious leaders. How pious they are! They live by the laws and keep all the feasts. You would think they would be good through and through, but it is not always so."

"I'm not talking about them, Father. I want to know about the men who call themselves prophets."

"It is the same for all men," Father said. "There are good and bad in all walks of life."

"But there must be a way to tell a good prophet from a bad one," John Mark insisted.

Father had put a comforting arm around his shoulders. "All I can tell you is to look into a man's eyes, John Mark. A man's true self is always there, deep in his eyes."

John Mark remembered his father's words as he hid behind the pile of cloaks. The Rabbi Jesus was talking to a man called Matthew. Matthew said something and Jesus nodded and smiled. It was the kind of smile you give someone when you are listening to what he is saying, but part of your mind is far away, thinking of something else. John Mark watched the lamplight flicker across the Rabbi's face. His eyes weren't at all wild or dangerous. They were kind, even gentle, but there was something else, something that John Mark couldn't catch. It wasn't until the conversation moved away from Jesus of Nazareth that he saw what it was.

Left alone for a moment, Jesus stared at the wall above John Mark's head. There was a lamp in front of him. The flame flared up, and the breath caught in John Mark's throat.

The Rabbi's eyes were spilling over with sadness.

A moment later a voice said, "Master?" and the look was gone. A question was asked by the man seated on his right. Jesus answered in a quiet voice and the conversation flowed around him again.

John Mark stared and stared. Nothing about the man from Nazareth was what he had expected. He wasn't clenching his fists or waving his arms around to make a point. He wasn't boasting or talking in a loud voice. He wasn't behaving like any of the other prophets John Mark had seen. Had this calm, sad-eyed man really attacked the moneylenders in the temple? It was hard to believe.

The hand washing was finished. What came next was the strangest thing John Mark had ever seen. The Rabbi Jesus got to his feet and wrapped a towel around his waist. He asked Rhoda to fill the bowl with fresh water. He took the bowl, knelt at the feet of the man on the next couch, and washed them.

The man looked so surprised John Mark was sure Jesus had never done such a thing before. He watched the rest of the men exchange amazed glances and knew he was right. When Peter's turn came, the fisherman pulled his feet away.

"You, Master, are going to wash my feet?"

John Mark forgot he was hiding from Rhoda. He forgot she was standing behind the Rabbi with a fresh towel. When he lifted his head so he could see better, his eyes met hers across the heads of the reclining men.

She glared at him. "What are you doing here?" she mouthed. "Out!" and stared pointedly at the door.

John Mark pretended he didn't understand her. Rhoda stared at the door again. There wasn't much else she could do without interrupting the foot washing ceremony.

John Mark stayed where he was. Sooner or later she would come and make him leave, but until then he would see everything.

A moment later the door opened. In came his mother. Rhoda indicated where he was with an angry toss of her head. Mother made her way over to him and whispered, "What are you doing here? Go downstairs."

The men didn't notice John Mark leave the room. They were too busy watching the scene between Peter and their master.

"I will never let you wash my feet!" Peter's defiant words followed John Mark down the stairs. At the bottom he stopped and listened, hoping to hear the Rabbi's reply, but his mother had closed the door. Frustrated, he sat down on the bottom step.

As John Mark sat on the moonlit staircase he thought about the preacher from Nazareth. He couldn't forget the look in his eyes. Why did he look so unhappy? Crowds flocked to hear him preach and see him heal the sick. He had friends like Peter and John, men who had given up everything to follow him. Who could ask for more than that?

It can't be because he is worried for his safety, John Mark decided. If he were afraid, he would have left Jerusalem days ago, and gone into hiding in Galilee. What can it be? What has happened to make him look so sad?

It wasn't very cold down in the sheltered courtyard, yet John Mark shivered. He moved closer to the house wall. He bent his knees and wrapped the skirt of his robe around his bare legs. He folded his arms against his chest but he didn't feel any warmer, for the chill was inside his body, not out. It was all so strange. After meeting Peter and John he had expected Jesus to be a bold, fearless leader, full of stories about the daring things he had done. John Mark had expected the mystery to clear up as soon as the Rabbi arrived. Instead, it was deeper than ever.

Lost in his thoughts, it was a moment before he realized the upstairs door had opened. Someone was coming down the stairs. It was Rhoda. As she passed him, he caught hold of her skirt. With a cry of alarm she almost dropped the bowl she was carrying.

She stared down at him, one hand to her heart.

"What are you doing lurking out here in the dark and

47

scaring me half to death?" she scolded.

"I'm sorry, I thought you saw me sitting here. What happened, Rhoda? Did Peter let the Rabbi wash his feet?"

Rhoda ignored him and went into the house. When she came out, she was carrying a bowl of parsley and a stack of unleavened bread.

"You had better keep out of the way, or your mother will be after you," she warned as she hurried by him.

When his mother came downstairs he had moved to the bench outside the downstairs door.

"Shall I carry some of the food upstairs for you?" he asked.

She shook her head. "Are you hungry?" she asked.

"Yes!"

The smell of roast lamb drifting out into the night was making his stomach rumble.

"I'll make supper for you. As soon as you have eaten it, I want you to go to bed."

"Bed? So early?" he protested. "I'm not tired. I don't want to go to bed yet."

"Then stop bothering us," she snapped. "If I have to say one more word to you . . . ." The rest of the threat was left unspoken as she hurried into the house.

6
I Spy

WHEN HIS MOTHER had gone back upstairs, John Mark leaned against the wall and stared gloomily up at the moon. It was at times like this he missed his father most of all. He was sure he would take his side.

"The boy is only trying to help." He could almost hear his father's deep rumbling voice.

It's hard, living with no man in the house, John Mark thought. And when I try to fill Father's place, Mother won't let me.

He had said as much to Rhoda one day when his mother was out. Rhoda had nodded in sympathy, but then she had taken his mother's side.

"You must understand about mothers, John Mark. For years they watch over their sons and worry about them. Then, because a boy reaches a certain age, his mother is supposed to stop worrying and let him be a man. That is hard to do. Harder for your mother because of your father's death. In a way, she is afraid to let you grow up. If you leave home, she will be alone."

John Mark had never thought of it that way before.

"You are always talking about being treated like a man, yet you don't act like one," Rhoda went on. "Remember what you and Samuel did to Martha on her way home from the well?"

John Mark grinned at the memory. Samuel's sister had been carrying a jug of water on her head. They had crept up behind her and tickled her. Of course she spilled the water. When they ran away she was standing there, soaking wet and howling with rage.

"She deserved it," he said. "She is so high and mighty. She's always making trouble for Samuel."

"So your answer was to play a childish trick on her. Was that the action of a man?"

John Mark had no answer.

"And what about the time I fell asleep under the grapevine and you tied me to it. Would a man do something so foolish?"

John Mark burst out laughing. "It was funny, Rhoda. If you could have seen your face when you woke up and found you couldn't move! You tried to stand, remember, and . . . ."

"Funny to you, maybe," she said sourly. "You were bored and you wanted to make mischief and I was a handy victim."

"Father did worse things when he was a boy," he reminded her. "You told me so yourself."

"When he was a *boy*," Rhoda countered. "I thought you wanted to be treated like a man?"

"I do. I'm the man of the house now."

"Then act like one."

"Mother won't let me. Whenever I try to help her, she brushes me off as if I were a fly that was bothering her," he complained. "Go to bed. Get up. Do this. Do that. I'm tired of it!"

"I didn't say it would be easy, John Mark. You must have patience. If you keep on trying to act like a man, your mother will soon see the difference."

"But you just said she doesn't *want* me to grow up," he had cried in frustration.

John Mark sighed as he remembered that conversation. Growing up was so complicated. Whatever he did seemed to be wrong. He thought about their Passover visitors. How wonderful it must be to be a grown man like Peter. To be able to leave home and travel around the countryside meeting all kinds of people. To be one of the small, brave band who followed the Nazarene wherever he went. What an exciting life Peter must lead!

If only I could be one of them, he thought dreamily. If only they would take me with them. I could run messages. Keep a lookout in times of danger. Maybe even save their lives!

It was a wonderful dream. And because John Mark had no idea what he was going to do with his life, it almost seemed as if it *could* happen.

When his father died, John Mark's mother had sold the family business. His father had been a merchant in the leather trade. Because of the bad smell, leather tanners had to work outside the city walls. John Mark's father bought cured leather from the tanneries and brought it into the city. He sold it to the shops that made sandals and bottles and other leather goods.

His mother had sold the business because John Mark wasn't old enough to take it over. The warehouse with its stock of leather had brought a good price. They had enough money to live on, but there was no trade for John Mark to follow.

He had enjoyed helping his father. Buying and selling was interesting work, but not something a boy could do.

John Mark knew how hard his father had worked to build up his list of customers. Being a good merchant was a matter of striking a good bargain and keeping your word. No man would bargain with a boy John Mark's age.

His mother was hoping John Mark's Uncle Barnabas would help decide his future. He lived on the island of Cyprus, a sea journey away from Israel. She had written to ask his advice. A few days ago they had received a reply saying he was coming to Jerusalem soon and would visit them.

Maybe he will take me back to Cyprus. John Mark thought. He grinned as he imagined telling Peter the fisherman about it.

"I'm going to Cyprus," he would say casually. "On a ship."

The Sea of Galilee was no bigger than a well when you compared it to the great sea Uncle Barnabas had to cross. John Mark was sure the ships that carried people to Cyprus made Peter's fishing boats look like toys.

The smell of roast meat drifted into his daydreams.

Food! he thought happily, and went indoors.

The heat from the fire had made the downstairs unbearably hot. To John Mark's bitter disappointment, his supper was the usual one of bread, olives, and cheese. He looked at the lamb on its spit. To one side was a pile of cut meat, ready to be taken upstairs. It looked delicious.

With a quick glance at the door, John Mark popped a tiny piece of meat into his mouth. It tasted wonderful, but as soon as he had swallowed it, he felt terrible. It wasn't *his* Passover lamb. He hadn't prepared for it. He hadn't said the required prayers. He hadn't taken part in the traditional washing of hands. He had no right to eat somebody else's sacred meal.

He took his supper outside. As he thankfully filled his lungs with cool air, he tried to decide where to eat it.

I daren't go up on the roof, he thought. There's nowhere up there to hide. If I want to stay up, I'd better keep out of the way.

There were plenty of shadowy places in the courtyard. Opposite the downstairs door was the olive tree. Between the tree and the courtyard wall, the shadows were thickest of all.

Back there I'll be safe, John Mark decided. Nobody will be able to see me, and I will have a good view of upstairs and down.

From his hiding place John Mark could see both doors and the staircase. As he ate, he watched his mother and Rhoda running up and down the stairs. Whenever the guest room door opened, the hum of voices became louder, but just as he caught a word or two, the door was closed again. Now and then the men's voices were raised in the words of a familiar Passover hymn. The rest of the time, one man seemed to be talking. It sounded like the Rabbi Jesus.

John Mark could still smell the roast lamb. It made his mouth water, even though his stomach was full. He was thirsty, but he didn't dare leave his hiding place for fear of coming face-to-face with his mother.

Once, when she passed Rhoda on the stairs, he heard her say, "Where is John Mark?"

"I haven't seen him," was Rhoda's reply.

As he knew she would, his mother searched the roof

53

next time she was up there. He chuckled and popped the last olive into his mouth. There was something exciting about hiding in the dark.

At long last the serving of the meal appeared to be over. Mother and Rhoda came downstairs, their hands full of empty bowls, and went into the family quarters and stayed there. John Mark could see them through the open door. They were washing the bowls and putting everything away. Upstairs the visitors were singing another hymn.

John Mark shifted restlessly. Hiding in the dark was fun, but he wanted to be up on the roof, listening to the man from Nazareth. Up there, he would be able to hear every word. The Rabbi might even come out onto the roof for air. Once or twice the guest room door had opened, and he had seen the outline of a man against the light.

If Peter came out, I could ask him why Jesus looks so sad, he thought.

Upstairs the hymn ended and there was silence.

Downstairs the two women were still working. John Mark groaned. Surely they must be finished by now! Why didn't they close the door and sit down and rest?

Close the door! he ordered them silently. Close the door so I can creep back up to the roof.

7
Secret Mission?

IT WAS WHILE JOHN MARK was waiting for the downstairs door to close that the man came out of the upper room. He turned to close the door, and the light caught his face. It wasn't the Rabbi, or Peter, or John. John Mark had seen him sitting close to Jesus, but he hadn't heard his name.

The man came down the stairs. John Mark thought he must be coming down to ask for more food or wine, but he stopped and put on his cloak. Halfway down he stopped again. This time he tugged at his headdress. He pulled the cloth forward and held it over the lower half of his face.

Back in the shadows John Mark frowned.

Why would he bother to hide his face on the streets at night?

The man reached the bottom of the staircase. He was about to turn the corner and pass the downstairs door when Rhoda came out of the house. Instead of stepping forward to speak to her, or pass her by, the man ducked back out of her sight. John Mark watched in amazement as he pressed himself against the house wall.

Rhoda hadn't seen him. She carried a bowl of water over to the jasmine bush and poured the contents around it. Back on the doorstep she put down the bowl

**He didn't move until Rhoda had gone back in-
doors. Why had he left before the others?**

and rubbed the small of her back. Behind her, John Mark could see his mother bending over the fire.

Rhoda stretched and looked skyward. "Did you see the stars, mistress?" she called. "It is such a beautiful night."

"I'm too tired to lift my head to look at anything," John Mark heard his mother say. "Come and help me put out the fire."

The man was standing so still John Mark thought he looked like one of the stone statues the Romans liked so much. He didn't move until Rhoda had gone back indoors. Then, one hand still holding the cloth over his face, he stole past the open door. As soon as he was safely past, he ran over to the gateway. With a quick glance over his shoulder, he slipped through the door and closed it behind him.

John Mark watched him go, his brain seething with questions. Why hadn't he wanted Rhoda to see him? Where was he going? Why had he left before the others?

There was only one explanation that he could think of. Jesus of Nazareth had sent him on a secret mission. John Mark stared up at the guest room, outlined against the inky blue sky. The murmur of voices rose and fell, but nobody was laughing. The feast didn't sound much like a joyous celebration of the Israelites' escape from Egypt.

"John Mark?"

He jumped. His mother was standing in the downstairs doorway. It was a moment before he realized she hadn't seen him.

"John Mark?" She called again, louder this time.

He held his breath.

"Where is that boy?" she said over her shoulder.

Rhoda appeared behind her. "I haven't seen him since he was sitting on the stairs," she said and went back to the fire.

John Mark started to laugh, then closed his mouth in case she noticed the flash of his teeth. The night is on my side, he thought with a shiver of pleasure. It has made me invisible.

"Answer me, John Mark!"

It was strange she couldn't see him. It wasn't as if he were hiding behind the tree trunk. If she walked in a straight line from the door to the wall, she would trip over him.

She stepped out into the courtyard and looked up at the roof.

"John Mark? Are you up there?"

I wish I could do this all the time, he thought. It's like being a spirit instead of a person. If I could do it in daylight I could go anywhere I chose. Nobody would be able to stop me. I'd spy on the Romans in their garrison. I'd walk past Pontius Pilate's guards and into his office. I'd even explore King Herod's palace and see if the stories about his treasures are true. It would be wonderful to be invisible. I could help people too! People like Jesus of Nazareth. I could go to the temple and find out what the priests are plotting and . . . .

With a guilty start he saw his mother had slumped down onto the bench outside the door. She looked so tired he wanted to run and throw his arms around her.

I'm playing another of those childish tricks Rhoda talked about, he thought. Hiding in the dark isn't something a man would do.

"I'm over here," he called. "Under the tree." He waved, and she caught the movement of his hand among the shadows.

"Come here this instant," she cried. With a quick glance at the upper room, she lowered her voice to an angry whisper. "Would you have me call you all night? Sometimes I wonder about you, John Mark. You never think. . . ."

John Mark groaned under his breath as the lecture went on and on. He knew he deserved it, but she didn't have to list everything he had done wrong since he was a baby.

It seemed as if his mother would go on all night. It was Rhoda who saved him. She came to the door, wiping her hands on a towel.

"Don't be too hard on him, mistress," she said. "It's not easy for a boy growing up without a father."

John Mark sent her a silent thank you. He loved Rhoda a lot. She was more like a member of the family than a servant. Sometimes, when she was in a good mood, she would sit with him and tell him stories of his father when he was a boy.

"You are like him in many ways, but he never plagued people with endless questions," she had told him many times. "Your father at your age knew how to hold his tongue, thanks be to God. Nobody I ever met asks as many questions as you, John Mark."

"I like to know things."

"Must you know *everything*?"

"I don't want to know everything," he protested. "I like to know about people, that's all. What's wrong with asking questions?"

"It is driving me into an early grave, that is what is wrong with it!" Rhoda always said the same thing, and they both smiled when she said it, for she was older than his mother.

Now, standing next to his mother, she said, "With God's help his curiosity will be put to good use one of these days."

"I hope so, Rhoda," Mother sighed. She frowned at John Mark and added the one word he was dreading most. "Bed."

"I'm not tired. Other nights you let me stay up much later than this."

"Tonight is different. I told you this morning I was worried for our guests' safety. I don't want to have to worry about you too, John Mark. I will feel much happier when you are in bed asleep."

All John Mark's good resolutions were forgotten. "I'm not a baby to be sent to bed just because you want me out of the way!" he cried.

"Aren't you?" she demanded. "What else would you call a son who hides in the dark and lets his mother call and call?"

"I. . . ." He groped for something to say in his own defense. "I didn't mean . . . I wasn't thinking. . . ." With a sheepish grin, he gave up. "I'm sorry."

Mother stood up and pointed to the door. "Bed. Now."

Indoors the fire was out, but it didn't seem to be any cooler.

"I'll never be able to sleep," he muttered to Rhoda.

She fanned herself with the towel.

"If only there was a breeze," she sighed.

"Anyone would think it was summer instead of spring, the way you two are complaining," Mother said briskly. "The house will cool down before morning."

"May I take my sleeping mat up to the roof?" John Mark asked. He often slept up there in warm weather.

"Not as long as our visitors are here," she said.

"When will they be leaving?"

"I don't know. Soon, I should think. Go to bed down here. If you are awake when they leave, you may take your mat up to the roof." She gave him a tired smile and kissed him. "May God watch over you this night, my son."

John Mark unrolled his mat and put it down close to the door. It was the coolest spot in the house. He took off his clothes and hung them on a peg. He lay down and covered himself with a sheet. By flapping the sheet he created his own breeze.

"That's better," he sighed.

John Mark rolled onto his stomach and peered out of the door. Opposite was the olive tree with its dark patch of shadows.

If somebody were there now I would never know unless he was dressed in white, he thought. He remembered how his brown robe had blended in with the shadows, hiding him from the man when he came down the stairs. The man's strange behavior was another part of the Passover puzzle.

Why was he acting as if he didn't trust us? he wondered. Mother is their friend. She risked a lot to let them use her guest room. If he was being sent on some secret mission, we wouldn't tell anybody.

He could still feel the heat from the fire. He wriggled

closer to the door as he watched his mother check the oil level in the lamp. Should he tell her about the man's strange behavior?

Better not, he told himself. She's too tired to be interested. She'll tell me to stop exaggerating and go to sleep. I'll tell her in the morning.

His mother put the lamp back into its niche in the wall.

"I'm going to sit outside on the bench," she said to Rhoda.

"Do you know where the Rabbi is going when he leaves here?" John Mark asked as she stepped over him.

"They said they were going somewhere quiet to pray."

"He's such a strange man," Rhoda said. "So . . . different. Nothing like I expected."

Nor me, thought John Mark.

8
More Questions

AS JOHN MARK LAY on his sleeping mat, he hoped his mother and Rhoda would fall asleep waiting for the visitors to leave. He had decided to creep back up to the roof. He wanted more than anything to hear what the man from Nazareth was saying.

The minutes passed. Mother's head was nodding. Rhoda was sweeping the hearth, stirring up clouds of ash that looked gray white in the moonlight.

"Aren't you tired?" John Mark asked her.

"Of course I'm tired!" was her sharp reply.

The longer John Mark waited for her to sit down, the more clearly he saw that what he was planning was wrong. When Rhoda had talked to him about acting like a man, he had listened, then forgotten her lecture.

Until today.

In the brief span of time since Jesus of Nazareth had walked into the courtyard, John Mark had thought over her words three times; when he was sitting on the stairs, back behind the olive tree, and again now, as he lay on his sleeping mat.

To defy his mother, that was bad enough. But how could he think of creeping up to the roof to listen to a private conversation? It would be like spying, and these men were guests.

John Mark felt himself go hot with shame.

If you don't have the courage to knock on the door and ask, then stay away, he told himself fiercely.

His body was damp with sweat. He gave the sheet a few shakes and rolled over.

"What happened upstairs after I left?" he asked Rhoda in a low voice. "Did Peter let the Rabbi wash his feet?"

"Not at first. They argued for a while and then Peter gave in."

"Did the Rabbi Jesus say why he was doing it?"

"He said something about setting an example for others. About servants and masters."

"Servants and masters? What did he mean by that?"

Rhoda put the broom in a corner and sighed. "I don't know, John Mark. I wasn't there to listen. I had work to do."

"You must have heard *something*," he insisted.

She reached for a dipper of water from the jar by the door and drank some. Before John Mark knew what was happening, she had poured the rest over his bare shoulders.

"That's for your questions!" she hissed.

John Mark grinned up at her as the cool water trickled down his back. "Please do it again," he pleaded. "It felt good."

"You!" she gasped. "You are impossible. One of these days...." She stepped over him and went outside. "That boy will question me into an early grave," he heard her mutter.

He heard his mother's soft laugh.

"Is it my son who has given you those gray hairs,

Rhoda? Come. Sit beside me and rest."

Leaning on his elbows, John Mark peered around the doorpost. "Do you think the Rabbi will stay in Jerusalem tonight?" he asked.

"Another question," Rhoda moaned and threw her apron over her head. "May God give us patience."

"We might as well try and stop the River Jordan from flowing," Mother said. "What is it this time, John Mark?"

He repeated the question.

"I hope not," she said. "It is much too dangerous here. Now that they have made a sacrifice and eaten the feast, I am sure they will leave. He would be much safer in Galilee."

John Mark could see the sense in that. Galilee was the Rabbi's home. He would be among friends there, and it was a good distance from Jerusalem.

"Mother? How did the Rabbi know about us? Who told him we have a guest room?"

"No more questions, please, John Mark." She sounded so weary he felt guilty. "Not tonight. I am too tired to answer them."

"Why don't you go to bed?"

"I can't go to bed until our guests have gone. How would it look if they came downstairs to ask for more food and found me asleep?"

"I'll stay awake. I'm not tired. You and Rhoda can go to bed. I'll wake you if they need anything."

"No thank you, my son. We can't go to bed. We are going to sit out here until they leave. Put out the lamp and go to sleep."

John Mark got up, blew out the lamp, and groped his way back to his mat. He was determined not to fall asleep. The voices overhead had suddenly become louder. Somebody must have opened the guest room door. John Mark waited, but there were no footsteps overhead, and nobody came down the stairs. Outside the door, his mother and Rhoda were discussing the meal they had just served and worrying whether there had been enough to eat.

In a few moments they fell silent. Upstairs, the men came to the end of a psalm, and someone began to speak. It was the Rabbi Jesus. John Mark stretched out on his stomach. He cupped his head in his hands and listened.

"What I command you is to love one another. If the world hates you, remember that it hated me before you. If you belonged to the world of evil people, the world would love you as its own. But you do not belong to the world, because my choice withdrew you from the world. Therefore, the world hates you. Remember. . . ." The words were cut off. Somebody had closed the guest room door.

"If the world hates you, remember it hated me before you," John Mark repeated the words in a whisper.

Is that why he looks so sad? he wondered. Is it because he thinks everybody hates him? He can't think that. *We* don't hate him, and there are a lot of people like us. He must mean the men in power, the chief priests and the Romans. They hate him, that's for sure.

It was impossible to make out anything else the Rabbi was saying. John Mark stared out at the courtyard.

The almond tree looked beautiful in the moonlight. Petals were drifting down like huge ghostly white raindrops. He recalled a conversation he had had with an off-duty soldier from the barracks at the Fortress of Antonia. The soldier had sworn he came from a country where rain was white in the winter time, and as soft as thistledown. Snow, he had called it. The conversation had reminded John Mark of something that had happened when he was very small. Early one winter morning, his mother had carried him up to the roof to show him a magical sight. The highest points of the city and the nearby hills were covered with a layer of white that sparkled in the morning sun. He remembered it was very cold. How excited everyone had been even though the whiteness was soon gone. It had been a dream, John Mark had thought until he met the soldier. Even now, he wasn't sure.

"Mother?" he called softly. "Is it true that. . . ?"

"Go to sleep, John Mark. Ask me tomorrow."

John Mark sighed. It was always the same. Tomorrow. Later.

How can I learn when nobody wants to answer my questions? he asked himself. Father never told me he was too busy or too tired.

John Mark thought about his father every day. With no man in the house to talk to, he often felt lonely. He had uncles and grown male cousins, but they lived too far away. He only saw them once or twice a year.

The rabbi who taught John Mark his lessons was willing to answer questions, but only if they were about the Jewish laws. After the trouble in the temple courtyard, John Mark had asked him about Jesus of Nazareth. The rabbi had looked shocked and had called Jesus a blasphemer.

"Isn't a blasphemer somebody who curses God?"

John Mark had asked. "Why is he a blasphemer?"

"Because he breaks the law."

"How?"

"In many ways. By working his so-called miracles on the Sabbath, for one!"

John Mark didn't understand how curing a sick person could be against the law. He knew it was against the law to work on the Sabbath. That made sense. But surely if a person were crippled or dying and somebody else could make that person better, it wasn't work. Not like digging a well, or building a house.

When he spoke up, his teacher's temper had flared. The rabbi had tugged at his beard and shaken his head. He said something about how it was a pity John Mark had no father to teach him the right way.

"What is the right way?" was John Mark's next question. It made the rabbi so angry he sent him home before the end of the lesson.

It was still hot in the house. John Mark started to feel drowsy. He swallowed a yawn.

Stay awake! he said to himself.

He wiped his face on a corner of the sheet and thought about the man from Nazareth.

I'll go and listen to him next time he preaches in the temple, he decided. If men like Peter give up everything to follow him, he must be somebody special.

9
Wake Up!

JOHN MARK MUST HAVE fallen asleep, for suddenly he heard voices close by.

The visitors were outside the door, talking to his mother. John Mark peered around the doorpost. Because their heads were covered, it was impossible to make out the Rabbi or Peter or John from the rest of the cloaked figures. There were twelve in all. He remembered there were supposed to be thirteen.

So that man didn't come back, he thought as he blinked himself awake.

"It is late," his mother was saying. "Why don't you stay until morning? You will be as safe here as anywhere."

One of the men thanked her. John Mark didn't recognize the voice.

"We are going outside the city to a garden to pray. To Gethsemane." John Mark recognized Peter's voice.

He waited for his mother to ask where they were going after that, but she only said. "May God go with you all."

"Blessings be upon you and your house," the men replied.

Rhoda stood up.

"Be seated, Rhoda." There was no mistaking Jesus' voice either. "We will let ourselves out."

John Mark watched them cross the moonlit courtyard. When the door in the gate closed behind them, his mother got to her feet and yawned. "Leave the upper room, Rhoda," she said in a low voice. "You can clean it in the morning. Let's go to bed."

"Shall I light the lamp or will it wake John Mark?" Rhoda whispered.

"I'm awake."

Rhoda gave a muffled cry. Mother laughed.

"Are you surprised?" she asked.

"You said I could take my mat up to the roof once they had gone," John Mark reminded her. "It is still too hot in here."

"Go. Go." Mother said. "Would you like to sleep on the roof, too, Rhoda?"

"I would, but my legs ache too much," Rhoda said. "They won't carry me up the staircase." She put her hand on John Mark's dark curly hair. "Sleep well, John Mark. May God watch over you this night."

"And you, Rhoda," he answered. He stood up and wrapped the sheet around his body. He kissed his mother good-night and ran up the staircase, dragging his mat behind him.

Up on the roof, he breathed in the cool night air and sighed with pleasure. Up that high he had a good view of part of the city. From the roof of the guest room it would be even better. He climbed up there and gazed out over the moonlit rooftops.

It was amazing how quiet it was for a holiday night. There was hardly anyone out and about. Here and there tiny pinpoints of light showed where people were still up. Out beyond the city walls he could see larger blobs of light. These were the campfires of Passover pilgrims who could find no place to stay in the city.

Inside the walls, the narrow streets were deep with shadows. Somewhere in that dark maze, the Rabbi Jesus and his followers were walking.

It was windy up that high, and much colder. John Mark wrapped the sheet around himself like a Roman toga. His eyes swept over the sleeping city until he found what he was looking for. Way down below he spotted a group of men crossing an open space between two buildings.

John Mark was sure it must be them. There were no other men out walking as far as he could see. Besides, they were heading for the gate that opened onto the Valley of the Kidron Brook. It was the one that would take them to the Garden of Gethsemane in the foothills of the Mount of Olives.

The men had disappeared into a dark tunnel that was a street below the market. John Mark watched and waited. He stared until his eyes ached, but he didn't see them again.

He climbed down to the main roof, aching with loneliness as well as with cold. He wished they hadn't gone. The house seemed so empty without them. With his bluff, outspoken personality Peter alone had filled the guest room.

I wish they had stayed the night, he thought sadly. I wish there had been time to get to know them.

He spread his sleeping mat in a sheltered corner and lay down. Out of the wind he didn't feel so chilled.

Just because Mother thinks they will go home to Galilee, it doesn't mean they will, he thought. Jesus isn't afraid of the priests, so why would he leave? Tomorrow I'll go to the temple and look for him.

The thought of seeing Jesus of Nazareth again made John Mark feel better. Listening to him preach would help to solve the puzzle. So would talking to his friends.

Peter must know why he looks so sad, he thought. I'll ask Peter.

He yawned once, and fell asleep.

*　　*　　*　　*

"Wake up!"

John Mark's eyes flew open. A figure was bending over him, shaking him awake. A cloud covered the moon, so it was too dark to see who it was.

"Wha . . . ?" A hand was clapped over his mouth.

"Keep quiet," a hoarse voice ordered. "If you cry out again I'll dangle you from the roof by your heels."

John Mark didn't recognize the voice. He started to struggle. From the weight of the body pinning him down he knew it was somebody his size.

He let himself go limp. "Samuel?" he mumbled.

The hand tightened.

"You haven't seen me tonight. Agreed?"

Now he knew it was Samuel.

He nodded. "I knew it!" he crowed when Samuel let him up. "I knew you would come if you suspected a mystery. I can always read your mind, Samuel."

"Lower your voice!" his friend hissed.

The cloud moved away and pearly white moonlight lit Samuel's face. To John Mark's surprise, he wasn't smiling.

He looks worried, he thought. Is it a trick of the light?

72

"What is the mystery?" Samuel whispered.

John Mark's teeth flashed in a wide grin. "The mystery is what will happen to you when your family discovers you are missing. No. It's no mystery. You will be beaten! Starved! Made to sleep with ten babies in one small room!"

Samuel bent and caught hold of John Mark's bare shoulders.

"Stop it! This is no time for jokes."

"Why not? Let go, Samuel. You're hurting me. What's the matter with you?"

"I want to know what is going on here tonight."

"*Was* going on."

"*Was*, then."

"A Passover feast, that's all."

Samuel frowned and let him go. "I don't understand," he said, half to himself. "Why would the temple police guards be interested in a Passover feast?"

"Temple guards? What are you talking about?"

"Who came to your house tonight?" Samuel demanded. "You must tell me, John Mark. It is very important."

John Mark had never seen him look so upset.

"It was a secret, but I suppose I can tell you now. It was Jesus of Naz . . . ."

"Jesus of Nazareth?" Samuel gasped. "So *that's* why the guards are coming here."

It was John Mark's turn to gasp. He stared at his friend in horror.

"Here? They are coming here? When?"

"They are probably on their way right now." Samuel stared down at the empty street. "I couldn't understand why they would want to come here, but of course if the Nazarene . . . ." He swung around. "Don't sit there gaping, John Mark! Don't you understand what I am telling you? The temple guards are on their way to arrest him!"

"Arrest him?" John Mark repeated stupidly.

I'm dreaming, he thought. In a moment I'll wake up and find it's all a dream.

"Yes! Where is the Nazarene? We must warn him."

John Mark struggled to pull his thoughts together. "He—he's gone. They have all gone."

"How long ago?"

"I don't know. I watched them leave and then I fell asleep. I don't know how long I slept. How late is it?"

"It is still the evening watch. You said "they." Was he here with some of his followers?"

John Mark nodded.

"How many?"

"Twelve."

"Twelve against so many!" Samuel said slowly. His voice was grim. "Where were they going?"

John Mark was wide awake now.

"To the Garden of Gethsemane."

"Gethsemane? That's near my Uncle Aaron's garden. Why were they going there so late at night?"

"They said they were going there to pray." John Mark caught hold of Samuel's arm. "How do you know the temple guards are coming here? Tell me, Samuel. Tell me!"

10
Clubs and Swords

I'LL TELL YOU in a moment," Samuel promised. "Which way did the Nazarene go?"

His voice was so urgent John Mark scrambled to his feet. He wrapped the sheet around himself and climbed up onto the guest room roof. "The last time I saw them they were passing the market. Come up here and I'll show you."

"That's the quickest way," Samuel murmured. "They will go out of the gate and along the Kidron Valley. That's the way we always go."

John Mark nodded. He had visited the garden belonging to Samuel's rich Uncle Aaron. Samuel and his family were allowed to use it in the summer when the city became unbearably hot.

"I wonder if they are there yet," he said.

They had no way of knowing, even though they could see beyond the city wall as far as the Mount of Olives. The Mount was a dark brooding hump against the starry sky. Except for the campfires, there were no other signs of life.

"How do you know the temple guards are coming here?" John Mark asked for the second time.

"I heard them say so," Samuel explained as they climbed back down to the main roof. "After I took the cooking pots to my grandparents' house I decided to come and see you. When we met by the perfume stalls you acted so strangely I knew something interesting was going on. I waited until after supper before I left. There were so many people there I knew I wouldn't be missed. I came by way of the street below the temple."

"Go on," John Mark urged. He felt suddenly colder and he hugged himself to keep warm.

"Outside the temple gate I saw a crowd of men carrying torches and lanterns. They were mostly temple police guards and some Roman soldiers. It looked as if there might be some kind of trouble, so I went closer. They were talking to a man about arresting Jesus of Nazareth. There was some argument going on. The man wasn't wearing a uniform, so I don't know who he was. I heard him shout, 'Do you want me to lead you there or not?' He mentioned your mother's name and your street, and I realized he was talking about your house!"

I *must* be dreaming, John Mark thought. He pinched the flesh of his underarm and winced at the pain.

It was no dream.

"Are you *sure* it was our house? There's a Mary one house from the corner."

"I'm sure," Samuel said. "Now that I know the Nazarene was here tonight, I'm doubly sure."

John Mark had never felt so confused. One half of his brain believed Samuel. The other half refused to accept the terrible news.

"The man was really nervous," Samuel went on. "I heard the police chief tell him to calm down; he would have to wait. The man said he had waited long enough. He said if he had known they would take so long he would have gone to the Romans. The chief said, 'I have my orders. We are not to proceed without official permission.' You know how they talk. The man wouldn't keep quiet. 'Whose permission?' he said. They said they were waiting for the chief priests. Someone had gone to wake them up. The guards were carrying clubs, John Mark, and the soldiers had swords." Samuel's voice shook.

John Mark's heart was thumping against his ribs.

"How long ago was this?"

"Not long. I didn't wait for the priests. I couldn't understand why they would want to send armed guards to your house, but I knew I had to warn you. I ran all the way." He lifted his head and listened. "Can you hear anything?"

There was no sound but the sleepy cooing of doves from a neighbor's dovecote.

"Maybe the chief priests wouldn't give their permission," John Mark said hopefully.

"That's impossible," said Samuel. "You know how long they have waited for a chance like this. Why didn't you tell me he was going to be your guest tonight?"

"I wanted to. Mother made me promise not to tell anybody. She said it was a secret."

"It wasn't a secret to that man, whoever he was," Samuel pointed out.

John Mark started to feel sick. He was glad the Rabbi and his friends had got away safely, but what would the guards do when they found they were too late?

"Is Mother asleep?" he asked Samuel.

"I think so. I whispered your name in the door and nobody answered. Rhoda was snoring. What are you going to do when they get here? Tell them where the Rabbi Jesus has gone?"

"Of course not!" The sick feeling grew stronger.

In the uneasy silence that followed, the two boys stood still and listened.

"If only . . ." John Mark said through chattering teeth.

"Sssssh! I think I heard something."

They listened harder.

"I don't hear anything," John Mark whispered. "I'm going downstairs to put on some clothes and wake my mother."

"Does she know where the Nazarene has gone?"

"Yes."

"Will she tell the guards?"

"My mother? Never!"

"What if they threaten to arrest her?"

"They can't. She hasn't done anything wrong."

"That won't stop them," Samuel said as he followed John Mark over to the staircase.

In his hurry, John Mark tripped over the hem of the sheet. For one horrifying moment he teetered on the edge of the roof.

"Help me," he gasped.

Samuel lunged for him and pulled him back.

"Thanks!" John Mark whispered as he bunched the sheet around his thighs. "When I've woken my mother and Rhoda, we'd better look for a place to hide."

It was too late. The boys were halfway down the stairs when a glimmer of light appeared at the end of the street. During ten heartbeats, the glimmer became bright torchlight. They watched in horror as a column of men swept around the corner and down the hill.

"Here they come!" John Mark cried.

Down the staircase the boys raced.

"Hide behind the olive tree. Quick!" Samuel gasped.

"I must wake Mother first!" The fear was tight in John Mark's throat.

Any moment the guards would be at the gate. Too late John Mark remembered that nobody had dropped the bar across the door after their Passover visitors had left. There was nothing to stop the men from marching into the courtyard. Should he bar the door first? Or should he wake his mother?

As John Mark hesitated at the bottom of the staircase. Samuel took charge. Using all his strength he dragged a protesting John Mark across the courtyard and behind the tree.

They were just in time.

The door in the gate opened and a guard, torch in hand, stepped into the courtyard. He unbarred the gate and swung it open. As John Mark and Samuel watched, terrified, the column marched in, torches held high, clubs and short swords at the ready. The only sounds were the thud, thud of their sandaled feet, the dull clank of armor against leather, and the hiss and splutter of the torches.

Light flooded the courtyard and the boys pressed themselves against the broad trunk of the olive tree. John Mark could feel the pounding of Samuel's heart against his bare shoulder. How glad he was that Samuel was there! It was bad enough to be caught naked and defenseless, but at least he wasn't alone.

There were Roman soldiers with the police guards, and behind them came other men. Some of them were wearing the robes of temple officials. They were carrying lanterns and their faces were hard and angry.

John Mark drew in a deep, ragged breath to shout a warning.

Once again Samuel clapped a hand over his mouth.

"Don't! She will be even more upset if they arrest you, John Mark. She would want you to hide."

He knew Samuel was right, but he felt like a coward all the same.

It was not as dark as the last time he had taken refuge there. A guard with a torch in his hand had taken up a position on the other side of the tree. He was so close the boys could have reached out and touched the metal studs on the back of his leather uniform.

As they waited for something to happen, John Mark realized they were trapped. With the courtyard so brightly lit and filled with armed men the only way out was over the high wall at their backs. How could they climb it without being heard?

He nudged Samuel with his elbow and pointed to the wall. Samuel shook his head, frowned, and pointed to the house. The police chief was at the door. He nodded to the captain of the soldiers, who raised his fist and beat upon it with a noise like thunder.

The sound echoed up and down the sleeping street. John Mark waited for doors to fly open, for neighbors to come rushing to their rescue. No one stirred. It was as if the city were in a deep, drugged sleep.

Even his own door stayed closed until the captain hammered on it again and shouted, "Open up! I order you, in the name of Caiaphas the high priest, to open this door!"

Slowly the door opened. Rhoda was standing there, fumbling with the belt of her robe. John Mark had never seen her look so afraid.

"Where is your mistress?" the captain bellowed. "Where is Mary?"

Rhoda's mouth opened, but no words came out. She put one hand on the doorpost, the other on her heart.

At the chief's signal, two guards took up positions on the stairs.

The captain raised his sword. "Answer me, woman!"

"I am here," a quiet voice said. "There is no need to wake the whole neighborhood. I am Mary. What do you want with me?"

John Mark's mother came out onto the doorstep. She had thrown a cloak over her nightshift. She had covered her head, but there had been no time to put up her hair. One long braid hung down over her shoulder.

"I hope you have good reason to wake us from our night's rest," she said coolly.

John Mark's heart swelled with pride. Only by the faintest tremor in her voice could he tell she was afraid.

"You know why we are here," the chief of the guards said. "Where is Jesus of Nazareth?"

As he spoke, John Mark's mother caught sight of the men on the stairs. Her eyes flickered toward the roof. The chief saw the look and misread it.

"So our information was correct," he said in a pleased voice.

"Search the roof, men," the captain barked. "Don't let him escape."

The guards sprinted up the stairs, torches in hand. "He's not here," they called down. "Nobody's up here."

"I hope you have good reason to wake us
from our night's rest," she said coolly.

John Mark saw his mother and Rhoda exchange a glance that was part relief, part puzzlement.

"Are you sure?" The chief frowned in disbelief.

"Looks like he *was* up here. Him and his friends. There's the remains of a Passover feast in the room."

"For how many?"

"I counted thirteen places."

The chief pointed to the downstairs door.

"Search in there, captain."

The captain pushed past Rhoda and disappeared.

"Nobody in there either, sir," he reported when he came out.

The chief's face was tight with anger. His eyes swept around the courtyard. They settled on someone standing in the shadow of the gate.

"You there," he said coldly. "You told us the Nazarene would be here. What do you mean by wasting our time?"

The chief was speaking to one of the men not in uniform. The boys hadn't noticed him before.

"You are the one who wasted time," the man snarled. "I told you we had to hurry. If you had listened to me you would have caught him."

The man stepped forward and somebody raised a lantern.

John Mark heard Samuel gasp.

"That's him!" Samuel breathed in his ear. "That's the man I was telling you about."

John Mark had gasped too. He stared at the man, his eyes wide with disbelief. The last time John Mark had seen him, he was stealing down the stairs, past Rhoda, and off into the night.

11
Samuel Goes Crazy

JOHN MARK'S mother and Rhoda had also recognized the man. They exchanged horrified glances.

"You sat next to him," Mother cried. "You broke bread with him. You are his friend."

Anger drove away Rhoda's fear. "*Was* his friend!" She spat the words out. "Would a friend betray you?"

The man backed away from the light. It was as if he thought the darkness would protect him from their accusing eyes.

"So you admit Jesus of Nazareth was here?" the chief said to John Mark's mother.

"What if he was?" she challenged him. "Where is it written that I am forbidden to lend my guest room for a Passover feast?"

Samuel dug his elbow into John Mark's ribs and flashed him an approving grin. John Mark didn't smile back. He was proud of his mother, but afraid for her too. The chief might take his anger out on her.

"Show some respect, woman," the captain growled.

"Respect!" Rhoda muttered loud enough for everyone to hear. "Where is the respect shown my mistress?"

"All we want to know is the whereabouts of the Nazarene," the captain said smoothly. "Maybe *you* would like to tell us."

Rhoda pursed her lips and stared at a tear in the sleeve of her robe. A temple official, proud and haughty in his brightly colored robes, walked over to the door.

"I don't think you understand," he said to John Mark's mother. "This is a serious matter. Jesus of Nazareth is wanted to face charges before the Sanhedrin."

"What kind of charges?"

"Serious ones. Too serious to be discussed with a woman," he sneered.

John Mark held his breath.

He's trying to upset her, he thought. Don't let him upset you, he pleaded with her silently.

"If the charges are not to be discussed with me, let me return to my bed," she said. John Mark felt his legs go weak with relief. "The man you want is no longer under my roof. There is nothing I can do. Come Rhoda."

She turned to go back in the house. The captain was too quick for her. His arm shot out and he blocked her way with his sword.

"Not so fast," he said. "You know full well there is something you can do. You can tell the chief what he wants to know."

The guards closed in around her. Back behind the olive tree John Mark whispered, "No!" and Samuel's hand, tasting of tree bark, was pressed over his mouth.

The nearest guard had also moved closer to the door. As soon as he was out of their hearing, Samuel whispered, "If they arrest her, will she tell?"

"Of course not! They will never find out from her. Or from Rhoda either."

"That man . . . that traitor might know."

John Mark nodded. "If I could be sure they weren't going to arrest my mother I'd try to escape over the wall and run and warn the Rabbi," he whispered in Samuel's ear. "Why don't you go instead?"

"I've never seen the Nazarene up close." Samuel whispered back. "How would I recognize him in the dark? I'll stay here with you."

If the chief thought they could frighten John Mark's mother into talking, he was mistaken.

"I am not a traitor to my friends," she said proudly.

The temple official smiled.

"So you admit the Nazarene is a friend of yours," he said.

He's trying to trick her, John Mark thought. Despite the night air and his lack of clothes, he started to sweat.

"I had never met him before tonight," she answered. "Now that he has been a guest in my house, I would like to think of him as a friend."

"You didn't know him before?"

"Not personally. Not to talk to face-to-face."

"Is that the truth?"

"Indeed, it is the truth."

John Mark leaned against the tree trunk and wiped his trembling hands on the sheet. It clung to his body with a clammy coldness that matched the fear in his heart.

"You are not one of his followers?"

"I told you I had never met him before."

"That doesn't mean you don't know where he has

gone," the temple official said.

"I agree," said the chief. He took off his helmet and wearily wiped his face on his forearm. "Come, woman, speak up so we can finish our night's work. Where did Jesus of Nazareth go?"

"I will tell you nothing. I am not the traitor here," she said. "Ask him. Ask the man who broke bread with the Rabbi and then betrayed him."

The chief looked around.

"Where is the man called Judas?" he asked.

Judas, thought John Mark. So that is his name.

"Come forward where I can see you," the chief ordered.

Judas stepped out of the shadows.

"Do you know where he has gone?" the chief asked.

As they waited for him to answer, Rhoda muttered something under her breath.

John Mark saw his mother put a warning hand on her arm.

Everyone was staring at the man called Judas.

"They were going outside the city to pray," he said. "It's not my fault you are too late. If you had listened to me he would be under arrest by now. I told you we had to hurry."

John Mark tugged at Samuel's sleeve.

"I am sure he knows," he whispered. "They won't bother my mother if he tells them. It will take a while for so many men to march to Gethsemane. I can get there faster. I'm going to climb over the wall and run and warn the Rabbi. You stay here and tell my mother I'm all right."

Samuel nodded.

"Wait until I've done something to distract the guards."

"Hurry," John Mark urged as he made sure the sheet was tied securely. Now that he knew what he had to do, he felt a surge of excitement. Better to do something than nothing!

"They were going to a garden," Judas was saying.

"A garden? At this time of night?" the temple official scoffed.

"Which one?" the chief asked. "The city is surrounded by gardens. It would take us days to search them all."

"It is his favorite place . . . ."

"Who does it belong to?" The chief sounded annoyed.

"A friend of his. Wait. The name will come to me . . . ."

"Here I go," Samuel whispered. "Watch me."

Silently he slipped out from behind the tree. Keeping well away from the pools of light he made his way around the courtyard. Two soldiers were guarding the gate. Both of them were listening to the conversation between the chief and Judas. Samuel crept up behind the nearest. He let out a yell and threw himself down on the ground. With another wild yell he rolled over and over until he was at the soldier's feet.

"Aaaaaaaeh . . . ." he cried, and wrapped his arms around the man's legs.

Caught by surprise, the soldier could only stare down at him in astonishment.

"What is it?" the chief called. "What's happening over there?"

"Aaaaaaeh!" Samuel wailed, and tightened his grip.

The soldier came to life and tried to kick himself free.

"Help! The boy is possessed by devils. Somebody help me!" In his desperation to free himself, the man dropped his torch, lost his balance, and fell over. With Samuel wailing, the soldier shouting, and the chief and the captain demanding to know what was going on, nobody heard John Mark scramble up and over the wall. He landed on his knees in the next-door courtyard. The sheet had come undone. As he retied it he saw the house door was partly open. Someone was there, watching and listening, but as John Mark hitched up the bottom of the sheet, the door closed and he heard a bar drop into place.

Nobody stopped him when he quietly unbarred the neighbor's gate and stepped out into the empty street. All up and down the hill doors closed so quickly he wondered if it was his imagination.

They've been listening, he told himself. They have all been listening but not one of them came to stand up for us.

John Mark had no time to be angry. Or to worry about having to run all the way to the Mount of Olives dressed in nothing but a sheet. Or to wonder what his mother would think of Samuel's strange behavior.

Back in the courtyard, Samuel was making more noise than ever. And so was the soldier.

"Get him away from me! He is possessed I tell you!"

Other voices joined in.

"Who is he?"

"Where did he come from?"

"Aaaaaaaeh . . . ."

"Let go of me you little . . . ."

"He must have slipped through the gate when we weren't looking."

"Calm down."

"Stop struggling, man."

"Aaaaaaaeh!"

The voices followed John Mark as he sprinted away down the hill.

12
John Mark on the Run

JOHN MARK TOOK THE shortest way to the gate that opened onto the Valley of the Kidron. With the sheet bunched up above his knees, he ran until he felt as if his lungs were on fire. In and out of the maze of streets and passageways he sped, skidding around corners and leaping over walls.

The first part of his desperate race was easy, even though clouds now covered the moon. He knew every pothole and rock in the streets around his home. Once, on a dare from Samuel, he had made his way to the market and home again, blindfolded. It had taken him longer than he had expected, but it hadn't been hard. He knew exactly how many steps there were in the steepest streets and the length of each passageway.

It was harder going in the streets beyond the market. He had to grope his way through darkness that was so thick he could almost feel it. Then the moon came out again, and it helped, but only in the open spaces. John Mark stubbed his bare toes on unseen steps and bruised his heels on half-buried rocks.

Once, he tripped over the sheet and tumbled down a short flight of steps. When he got up, he could feel blood trickling down his legs. It was too dark to see the damage. He retied the sheet and set off again, limping badly.

Every so often, John Mark had to stop to ease the burning pain in his side. Over the pounding of his heart, he listened for the sound of marching feet. He heard nothing. The city was so quiet he began to wonder if he had imagined the scene in the courtyard.

You didn't hear them coming then, he reminded himself. Why would you hear them now?

Not everybody in Jerusalem was asleep behind barred doors. John Mark passed cloak-wrapped figures half hidden in doorways or slumped against walls. The still, silent figures terrified him. Were they sleeping, or were they dead? He raced by, propelled by a fear of being attacked by one of these faceless strangers.

He was more than halfway to the gate when he took what he thought was a short cut down some steps. The other end was blocked by a fallen building. It was a dangerous part of town, one where he would normally never go after sundown. It was a long climb back to the top, so he turned down a passageway. The way was pitch dark and so narrow he could touch the walls on either side. He stepped on something wet and slimy, and a foul smell made him choke.

There were no human sounds in the dark place. Unseen animals, disturbed by his coughing, scuttled by.

Rats! Fear curdled John Mark's stomach as he thought of his bare, bleeding legs. His trembling hands touched a rotting doorframe. He wrenched a piece of

**The still, silent figures terrified him.
Were they sleeping or were they dead?**

wood out of the frame. Using it to sweep the ground around his feet, he backed out of the passageway.

John Mark had lost precious time. At last he reached the gate in the city wall and sprinted through it. There was no sign of a guard on duty, but he didn't slow down.

The road outside was lined with tents. Wrapped in cloaks and blankets, people were huddled around campfires. Some of them looked up as John Mark ran by, doubled over and gasping for air.

He waited until he was well clear of the camps before he stopped to catch his breath. To his relief, there was no sign of anyone following him. He was about halfway to the Garden of Gethsemane. Crossing the Valley of the Kidron would be easier because it was open, but he still had a long way to go.

The valley was ghostly gray in the moonlight. Its stony slopes were scattered with tombs. The Kidron wasn't big enough to be called a river. Most of the year it was dry, but now, in spring, there was water in it.

At a steady trot John Mark followed a path that ran alongside the stream. He was less afraid now that he was out of the city. Out in the open he would know when the guards were catching up.

Halfway along the valley John Mark stopped and looked back. There was no sign of anybody, so he decided to rest for a moment. He kept away from the shadowy tombs and sat down on a rocky wall. In the bright moonlight he examined his legs. The blood had dried to a thick crust. His feet were covered with evil smelling mud. It was impossible to tell if they were bleeding too. It won't take a moment to wash them in the Kidron, he decided.

He climbed down the bank with its spring growth of soft grass and waded into the water. Bending, he scooped up a handful to wash the dust from his mouth. As it ran through his fingers he saw it was dark colored. He scooped up some more, and stared at it.

"Why does it look so dark?" he wondered out loud.

With a shiver, he remembered. It wasn't a trick of the moonlight. It was blood! The stream wound close to the temple outer wall. A channel had been built from the altar, out through the wall. It was used to carry away the blood of the sacrificed animals. The channel emptied into the Kidron. At times of celebration, like Passover, it was used every day.

John Mark knew all about sacrifices. The law said they had to be made and everyone tried to live by the law. Yet the sight of the blood-dark water flowing around his ankles struck terror to his heart.

What if it is human blood? he thought wildly. What if it's the blood of the Rabbi and his friends? What if I'm too late?

He splashed out of the murky water. His feet felt as if they were slippery with blood. With a handful of sand he scoured his legs and feet until they stung. The pain brought him to his senses.

The temple guards couldn't possibly be there before me, he told himself. Not unless they sprouted wings and flew over the walls. I came by the shortest and quickest way.

He leaped across the bloody water and ran to the top of the nearest slope. There was no sign of movement anywhere in the valley. No column of marching men. No lights, except those of the distant campfires.

The valley looked peaceful and yet the skin was prickling on the back of John Mark's neck. The Kidron ran with blood and the dead of long ago lay buried in the tombs. Who knows what unearthly spirits had watched him pass by?

He was glad he had reached the foothills of the Mount of Olives. It wasn't far now. If the guards marched out of the city at that very moment, he was sure he would have time to run and warn Jesus of Nazareth.

Every part of John Mark's body ached as he limped along, but he didn't care. He had beaten the guards. The Rabbi Jesus and Peter and John would have time to escape. That was all that mattered.

He came to an olive grove and stopped and looked back. The moon hung in the sky like a silver-colored fruit. The light it shed was almost as bright as day. John Mark could make out details in the stone work of the city wall. His eyes followed the wall to where the arches over the gateway stood out against the night sky.

Where are the guards? he wondered. Why are they taking such a long time? Did Judas give them the wrong name?

He felt a surge of hope.

He didn't say anything about the garden being below the Mount of Olives. Maybe he sent them in the wrong direction!

"You had better warn the Rabbi all the same," he said out loud. "The guards won't give up. Not when the chief priests sent them."

There was a biting wind blowing along the valley. Now that he had stopped running, John Mark was trembling with cold. He wrapped the sheet around his shoulders and limped into the olive grove.

It was a pity he turned his back on the valley just then. A moment longer and he would have seen a frightening sight. Flowing out of the city gate like a stream swollen by winter rains came a column of men far bigger than the one that had marched on his mother's house.

Armed with clubs and swords, trailed by a mob they had gathered along the way, the guards and soldiers tramped toward Gethsemane with incredible swiftness.

13

To Interrupt or Not

AFTER THE BRIGHTNESS of the open valley, it seemed dark under the trees. John Mark, warmer since he was out of the wind, made his way from one patch of moonlight to the next.

He came out of the other side of the olive grove and found himself on a path. The path, as pale as newly washed sheep's wool, was much easier to follow.

The foothills of the Mount of Olives were scattered with gardens. Most of them belonged to families who lived in Jerusalem.

John Mark limped past walled gardens full of apricot and almond trees in full bloom. There were fig trees, too, and here and there a solitary palm tree towered overhead. He sniffed at the fresh, sweet night air. It smelled of spring. It was a pleasant change from the city smell of people and animals and cooking.

John Mark was sure he knew the way, yet he was amazed how different the paths looked at night. Every tree, every plant, every stone was lit with a strange silvery glow. He found it hard to tell one garden from the next. Twice he took a wrong turn.

At last he found Samuel's family garden. He recognized it by the tree next to the gate. When they were small, he and Samuel had spent many hours sitting up in that tree. Sometimes they spied on the people who passed by. Sometimes they pretended it was a fort they were defending against the Romans. The rope swing Samuel had made for his sisters was hooked over one of the branches.

Past the garden there was a ravine he would have to cross. He came to it and hesitated. The bottom was lost in darkness.

Go around it, he told himself. You have plenty of time.

It took longer than he had thought. At last, up ahead, he saw a cluster of date palms outlined against the star-sprinkled sky.

It's just past those palms, he thought with a sigh of relief.

John Mark's step quickened. He came to a wall and followed it around a corner. The Garden of Gethsemane lay directly ahead.

At the gate he stopped to listen. In the distance, a dog was barking. Closer, a donkey brayed, and another answered it. The dry rustle of palm leaves filled the air.

I don't hear voices, John Mark thought. Maybe they have gone. But why would they come all this way to pray and not stay a while?

The Garden of Gethsemane was much bigger than the garden that belonged to Samuel's Uncle Aaron. There were more trees. John Mark opened the gate and looked around. He couldn't see anybody.

He walked deeper into the garden and stood still. Somewhere up ahead a man's voice broke the stillness. It sounded like Jesus of Nazareth, but John Mark couldn't tell if he was talking to his friends or praying. He looked down at the sheet, and his face burned.

It's bad enough to interrupt a rabbi at his prayers, but to do it dressed like *this*? Why didn't I ask Samuel to lend me his robe?

As he stood there, an idea came to him.

I'll hide behind something and call out and tell them why I'm here, he decided. I can show my face so Peter and John will know it isn't a trick. I hope they will believe me.

John Mark kept to the shadows as he made his way toward the sound of the Rabbi's voice. Up ahead, through the trees, he could see the bulky shape of an olive press. The great, round stones shone white in the moonlight.

The voice sounded as if it were coming from somewhere beyond the olive press. John Mark reached the last tree. He hitched up the bottom of the sheet and dropped to his knees. Slowly he crawled over to the press and hid behind the big, vertical stone wheel that was used to crush the olives.

He sounds as if he's praying, John Mark thought. I can't interrupt him at his prayers.

He sat down on the stone platform and tucked his hands in his armpits. The cold seeped through the sheet and he started to shiver again. His teeth chattered. He rocked to and fro and thought with longing of his warm, wool cloak hanging on a peg at home.

As John Mark sat there, he couldn't help hearing every word Jesus spoke.

"Abba, Father, everything is possible with you."

John Mark sat still. Abba? The word echoed in his head.

So he isn't praying after all, he thought. He's talking to his father. I didn't know his father was with him.

He stood up and peered around the wheel. There in a small clearing lit by moonlight, Jesus of Nazareth was kneeling. His head was bowed and he was alone.

I'm sure I heard him say "Abba," John Mark thought, puzzled. If he is talking to his father, where is he? And where are Peter and John and the others?

As John Mark stared at him, the Rabbi lifted his head.

"Take this cup from me." There was pleading in his voice. His head dropped again. "But let it be as you, not I, would have it." The last words were like a sigh.

John Mark frowned.

He *is* praying, he thought. He must be. There is nobody else here. But why is he calling God, Abba? That's what I used to call my father. It's the name all children use.

There was a hush in the garden so intense, John Mark held his breath.

Jesus seemed to have finished praying, for he got to his feet. John Mark wanted to call out to him, but he didn't dare break the silence. He watched the Rabbi walk over to the far side of the clearing and bend over something on the ground.

"Simon Peter, are you asleep?" The words carried easily to where John Mark was hiding.

It was only then that he saw there were cloak-wrapped figures stretched out among the shadows under an olive tree. There were three of them, and they were sound asleep.

"Were you not able to stay awake for one hour?" Jesus was asking as he tried to wake them. "You should

101

be awake and praying not to be put to the test."

The men slept on. Jesus turned away.

"The spirit is willing, but the flesh is weak," he said sadly.

John Mark watched him walk back into the center of the clearing. He thought of the Passover feast in his mother's guest room. He remembered the look in Jesus of Nazareth's eyes. He had looked sad then, surrounded by friends. How much more unhappy he must feel now, all alone in the night with not one person to keep him company! John Mark thought of his mother, sitting on the bench outside the door. Tired as she was, she had stayed awake. If she could do that for her guests, couldn't Peter and John do as much for the man they called Master? And where were the rest of his friends? Out of so many, couldn't *one* keep watch with him?

John Mark could tell the Rabbi was upset by the way he dropped to his knees.

He started to pray again. He used exactly the same words as before. He called God "Abba" as though he were a child talking to his father. He was in such agony that when he lifted his head, drops of sweat as dark as blood ran down his face. John Mark felt as if a giant hand were squeezing his heart.

I'm here! You're not alone! he wanted to shout. But he didn't dare voice the words.

Once again, Jesus stood up and walked over to the tree. His voice sounded more urgent this time. When he tried to wake the men, all three stirred. Two tugged at their cloaks and turned over. The third lifted his head. John Mark was too far away to be able to tell if it was Peter. He murmured something and fell back to sleep.

The Rabbi waited, but none of them moved again.

He walked back to the center of the clearing. His steps were slower, as if he, too, were tired. John Mark felt as if he couldn't bear to listen to another word.

This time, when Jesus fell to his knees the moonlight seemed much brighter.

"Abba, Father, everything is possible with you.... Take this cup from me...."

John Mark's eyes filled with tears. He had never heard anybody sound so lonely. Who was this man from Nazareth? Was he really the Son of God? Who else would talk to God and call him Abba? But if God was his father, why wasn't he answering him?

And why were none of the Rabbi's friends with him? How could they sleep when he needed them?

John Mark wiped the tears away with a corner of the sheet. When he looked up, the light had dimmed, even though there were no clouds near the moon. Under the olive tree, the men were still asleep.

I'll wake them! he vowed. If I circle around the clearing the Rabbi won't see me.

He was about to make a dash for the nearest tree when Jesus stood up. This time, he walked briskly over to the olive tree.

"You can sleep now and take your rest," he said. "It is all over. The hour has come." He lifted his head as if he had heard something. "The Son of Man is betrayed into the hands of sinners."

John Mark stared. His voice was different. It didn't sound at all unhappy.

What happened? he asked himself. Was it something to do with the light?

103

Jesus bent over the sleeping figures and shook them.

"Get up!" he ordered. "Let us be going. Look! My betrayer is here."

The men stood up, and John Mark saw one of them was Peter. Moments later, lights appeared through the trees. The gate clicked. The three men were still stretching and yawning when the first of the temple guards, clubs at the ready, came rushing into the garden.

14
Undone!

OVERWHELMED BY GUILT, John Mark pressed himself against the cold stone of the olive press and stared, terrified, at the advancing guards.

Why did I wait so long? If they arrest him it will be my fault. I should have warned him and now it is too late!

His eyes filled with bitter tears as he turned to look at Jesus. The Rabbi stood facing the gate, calmly waiting.

"The hour is come ... my betrayer is here," John Mark repeated the words in a whisper as he blinked the tears away. "He *knew* they were coming to arrest him. He knew, and yet he didn't run away."

There was no time to wonder why. Or to wonder how the guards and soldiers had covered the length of the Kidron Valley so quickly. They were in the garden, and they had changed. The disciplined columns of men who had marched into his mother's courtyard had become a mob. Their eyes gleamed in the torchlight. Followed by rough-looking men with sticks and boys with rocks in their hands, they looked more like wild animals stalking their prey.

The acid taste of fear filled John Mark's mouth. Not for himself, but for the man who stood alone in the clearing. Nobody had noticed John Mark. The guards halted. All eyes turned to the path that led to the gate.

It was Judas they were waiting for. He came into the clearing with the police chief.

John Mark's fists clenched. He stared at Peter.

Do something! The words screamed inside his head.

Peter and the other two were huddled together under the tree. Beyond them, among the trees, John Mark could dimly see the outlines of other cloaked men. If they were the rest of the Rabbi's followers, they made no attempt to rescue him.

Soldiers were sent back to guard the gate. The priests and the rest of the mob lined up behind the guards. Two boys not much older than John Mark ran over to the olive press.

"We'll have the best seats in the arena," one laughed. His breath smelled of sour wine as he pushed past John Mark and climbed onto the platform.

Jesus had made no attempt to escape, yet the captain ordered his men to keep their swords ready. The chief turned to Judas.

"Well?" he said. "We are waiting."

Judas looked at Jesus.

"Rabbi!" he cried, as if surprised to see him standing there. Arms outstretched in greeting, he walked toward him. Jesus didn't move as Judas put his arms around him and kissed him.

John Mark gasped to see the traditional kiss of friendship and respect put to such use. He clung to the stone wheel, sick with disgust.

"That's him all right," one of the boys chuckled as the chief and the captain exchanged pleased glances.

"Judas," Jesus said. "Are you betraying the Son of Man with a kiss?"

Judas turned away.

"Arrest the Nazarene!" the captain ordered.

The guards rushed toward him. The priests and temple officials hurried after them, lanterns swinging, their faces alight with triumph. It was only then that Peter came to life. He flung back his cloak. "Lord, shall we use our swords?" he cried.

Without waiting for an answer, he pulled out his short sword and rushed to the rescue. John Mark silently cheered him on. At least Peter was doing something!

Peter launched himself into the crowd around Jesus. With one wild sweep of his sword he cut off the ear of a man dressed in the uniform of a temple servant. Two soldiers, their swords flashing in the torch light, drove Peter back.

They had unexpected help from their prisoner.

"No more of this," he called to Peter. "Put away your sword. Am I not to drink the cup my father has given me?"

He reached out, touched the servant's ear, and it was healed.

The mob's blood lust was too powerful for them to notice the miracle. John Mark saw it and gasped out loud. Who but the Son of God could do such a thing? And if he could replace a man's ear with a touch, surely he could free himself if he wanted to.

If he wanted to.

There were no more miracles. Except for Peter, driven back to the tree on the point of a sword, Jesus was alone. The rest of his followers had disappeared into the night.

The guards bound his hands behind him.

"Do you take me for a robber that you come with

swords and clubs to arrest me?" he asked. "Day after day I sat teaching in the temple and you didn't lay hands on me. But let the Scriptures be fulfilled."

He made no resistence when the guards started to drag him away. Many of the mob were laughing and cheering. The two boys leaped from the olive press with delighted yells. When John Mark looked for Peter, he couldn't believe his eyes. Peter, his one bold gesture over, was running toward the back wall of the garden. John Mark watched him vault over it and disappear.

"Twelve against so many," Samuel had said. It was one against so many and it wasn't fair! Rage boiled up inside him. Powered by it, John Mark raced after the guards.

The detachment, with Jesus in the middle, had reached the gate when John Mark caught up with them. A soldier was opening it to let them out. One of the guards gave Jesus a push to hurry him. The push, impatient and uncaring, was so hard Jesus lost his balance and staggered against the gatepost. John Mark heard him gasp. Unable to use his arms to protect himself, his stomach had taken the full impact of the post. The look of pain on the Rabbi's face was more than John Mark could bear. The rage boiled over, and all caution left him.

"You cowards!" he yelled. "Leave him alone!"

Surprised faces turned in his direction.

"Who is this boy?" the captain demanded.

"Not another one," the chief groaned. "Is every boy in Jerusalem possessed by evil spirits tonight?"

"This one has no clothes so it must be a cold spirit," somebody joked and the men laughed.

As he struggled to free himself, John Mark looked
to where Jesus was standing, his arms bound,
his cloak trailing in the dust.

"I said leave him alone!" John Mark threw himself in front of Jesus.

Rough hands caught hold of him and dragged him away. John Mark kicked and squirmed but his captor was too strong for him. As he struggled to free himself, John Mark looked to where Jesus was standing, his arms bound, his cloak trailing in the dust. Their eyes met. Jesus was looking at him with such understanding, John Mark felt his rage draining away.

"What shall we do with the boy, sir?" the captain asked.

"Arrest him!" The chief sounded angry. "I've had enough for one night. Lock him up until he learns some respect."

John Mark's captor called for some rope. He loosened his grasp as he reached for it. Wriggling like a fish out of water, John Mark was free.

"Look out, Marcus!" a voice called and a hand caught hold of the back of the sheet. A sharp tug, and the knot came undone and John Mark was free of it.

"Close the gate!" the captain ordered.

John Mark dodged between two soldiers and around a guard. The guard swung a club at his head and missed. Through the garden John Mark raced. Cursing, two of the soldiers gave chase. They were hampered by their armor and he easily outdistanced them. Barefoot and naked, he was like a pale shadow as he slipped in and out of the trees.

John Mark was scrambling over the back wall when he heard a voice call, "Marcus? Let him go. The chief says we are wasting time."

Crouched against the far side of the wall, he heard the

men drop back. He waited a few moments before getting to his feet. Shivering with cold and fear he started to run.

He made his way to the only place he could think of.

The garden belonging to Samuel's Uncle Aaron.

It was there, huddled in a corner behind a stack of empty water jars, that Samuel found him.

15
Mystery Fulfilled

JOHN MARK?"

John Mark had no idea how much time had passed before he heard the familiar voice calling his name. He was too numb with horror at the scene in the garden to be able to think clearly.

"John Mark, are you here?"

He staggered to his feet, stiff with cold and aching all over.

"I'm over here. Behind the water jars."

Samuel's cloaked figure came running down the path.

"What are you doing back there?"

"Hiding. And trying to keep warm. I'm naked."

"Here's your cloak." Samuel tossed it to him. "Your mother made me bring it."

"Is she all right?" John Mark asked anxiously.

"Yes. They didn't bother her once Judas remembered the name of the garden."

"And you? What did they do to you?"

"Nothing much. They thought I was possessed. Your mother told them I lived in the neighborhood and she would take care of me, and so they left. I managed to delay them for a while," he said proudly. "I wish you had seen me! It took four men to make me let go of that soldier's legs. I managed to get free of them and I ran round and round the courtyard. Then, when they finally caught me I thrashed around so much and screamed and wept and wailed they forgot all about Judas." He stopped and stared at John Mark. "Whatever happened to you? You are covered with scrapes and bruises. And where is the sheet?"

"They took it."

"They?"

"The guards."

"Did they beat you?" Samuel asked as John Mark thankfully wrapped himself in the heavy, wool cloak.

"No, they were too busy," he said bitterly. "They arrested Jesus of Nazareth."

"I know. I passed them on their way back into the city. I hid behind a tomb in case they recognized me. They were acting as if they had caught the worst murderer in the world."

"How did he look?"

"They were forcing him to run, and he kept stumbling, but I didn't hear him complain. Were you too late to warn him? I thought I gave you plenty of time."

"I did have enough time," John Mark slumped against the wall. "He was praying when I got there. I waited, and then it was too late. I felt terrible. I *still* feel terrible but. . . . ." His voice trailed away and he stared up at the moon.

"But what?" Samuel said.

"But I wasn't the only one who knew they were coming after him. *He* knew, but he didn't stop them."

"Stop them? How could one man stop a mob like that?"

"The Son of God could. The Messiah."

Samuel tapped his forehead. "Are you sure you didn't fall and hit your head?"

"He *is* the Son of God, Samuel. I know it now. I heard him call God "Abba," and I saw a miracle. Peter cut off a man's ear with his sword and Jesus healed it."

"Then why didn't he work another miracle to save himself?" asked the practical Samuel.

"I don't know why," John Mark said with a sigh. "It's all such a mystery."

"Tell me everything that happened," said Samuel. "To start with, who is Peter?"

They sat with their backs against the wall. In that sheltered spot, warm for the first time in hours, John Mark told Samuel everything that had happened from the moment Peter and John came to his house.

When he had finished, Samuel shook his head. "It still doesn't make sense, John Mark. If the Nazarene is the Messiah, why did he let himself be arrested and dragged away like a common criminal?"

John Mark shrugged.

"He has always outfoxed the chief priests before. Why would he suddenly give up?"

"There's a reason; I know there is," John Mark said. "It's all part of the mystery. When he was praying he said something about the Scriptures being fulfilled. About it being God's will that was done, not his own. As if he had no choice. Like when your father tells you to do something and you don't want to, but you do it anyway because there has to be a reason." He drew in a deep breath. "I think he knew all along that he was going to be arrested tonight! That's why he looked so sad earlier."

114

"Why would he let it happen if he had the power to stop it? Everyone knows the chief priests would like to see him dead."

"Maybe he wants to wait until the trial," suggested John Mark. "If he worked some miracle to free himself in front of the Sanhedrin, the whole world would hear about it!"

"He will need a miracle," said Samuel. "They will never let him go."

He stood up and hauled John Mark to his feet. "I promised your mother I would bring you home as soon as I found you. She said she was going to wait up."

They started the long walk back along the valley. Samuel slowed his pace so his footsore friend could keep up. As John Mark limped by the bloody waters of the Kidron, he thought of Peter.

Where did he go? he wondered.

He was sure Peter hadn't run away for good. Not Peter.

I wish I could find him and talk to him, he thought as he pulled the cloak closer.

There were so many unanswered questions!

What did it mean to be a fisher of men? How did you become a follower of Jesus of Nazareth? Was there something you had to do first?

The two boys left the moonlit valley and entered the sleeping city. As they made their slow, silent way through the narrow streets, John Mark came to a decision.

"I'm going to follow him," he said out loud.

Samuel stopped.

"Follow who?"

"Jesus of Nazareth. When I'm old enough I'm going

115

to be a follower like Peter."

"Oh, John Mark," Samuel sighed. "The chief priests have arrested him. He will never get out of their clutches alive, you know that. You will never see him again."

"I don't believe it," John Mark said stubbornly. "He's the Son of God, Samuel. He let himself be arrested for a reason. Sooner or later we will find out what it is."

"How can you be a follower when you've never heard him preach?"

"I heard a little of what he said in the upper room tonight. Peter told me he hates injustice, and so do I."

"But...."

"I've seen him, Samuel. That's all that matters for now." Suddenly, all John Mark's aches and pains were gone. He strode ahead so fast Samuel had to run to catch up with him. "I'm going to do it, Samuel. You wait and see."

*   *   *   *

And he did. As a young man he became a member of the early Christian church. He became friends with Peter. Late in Peter's life he wrote down the apostle's words and they became the Gospel of Mark.

He had many adventures as one of the first missionaries. He joined his Uncle Barnabas from Cyprus and the apostle Paul on their travels when they risked their lives to preach the gospel of Jesus Christ to the world.

But that is another story.

The Author

Ann Bixby Herold was born in England, just outside London. From the age of eight, she wanted to see her name on the cover of a book. She also wanted to travel around the world. The latter proved easier!

In her late teens and twenties she lived and worked in Norway, Cyprus, Central Africa, Spain, Germany, New Guinea, and finally Bermuda, where she met her future husband, Horst.

After marriage they settled in Pennsylvania. House-bound with a baby, she began writing for women's periodicals in Great Britian. When Mattias grew to reading age, she wrote children's stories for him and for magazines. Her boy was ten before her first book was published.

Raised as an Anglican, she belongs to Good Shepherd Episcopal Church in Hilltown, Pennsylvania. She has been a member of the vestry, is a lay reader, and led the adult Sunday school for three years.

She teaches the writing of American historical fiction and creative writing. When visiting schools, she often dresses in 17th-century Quaker costume and talks about colonial America. She also lectures to adult groups.

Herold has published *The Helping Day, Phoebe Moon's Pocket, Aaron's Dark Secret,* and numerous stories.